Hook Up

Also by Kim Firmston
In the SideStreets series:
Schizo

Hook Up

Kim Firmston

James Lorimer & Company Ltd., Publishers
Toronto

James Lorimer & Company Ltd., Publishers acknowledges the support of the Ontario Arts Council. We acknowledge the financial support of the Government of Canada through the Canada Book Fund for
our publishing activities. We acknowledge the support of the Canada
Council for the Arts which last year invested $24.3 million in writing
and publishing throughout Canada. We acknowledge the Government
of Ontario through the Ontario Media Development Corporation's
Ontario Book Initiative.

Cover image: iStockPhoto

Library and Archives Canada Cataloguing in Publication

Firmston, Kim
    Hook up / Kim Firmston.

(SideStreets)
Issued also in electronic format.
ISBN 978-1-4594-0030-6 (bound).--ISBN 978-1-4594-0029-0 (pbk.)

    I. Title. II. Series: SideStreets

PS8611.I75H66 2012   jC813'.6   C2011-907311-0

James Lorimer & Company Ltd.,   Distributed in the United States by:
Publishers   Orca Book Publishers
317 Adelaide Street West, Suite 1002   P.O. Box 468
Toronto, ON, Canada   Custer, WA USA
M5V 1P9   98240-0468
www.lorimer.ca

Printed and bound in Canada.
Manufactured by Friesens Corporation in Altona, Manitoba, Canada in
February 2012.
Job #72988

Chapter 1

"Hey Manywounds!" Adam Blake calls out, striding to meet me. "Is that how you're going to look after I'm done with you?"

I grin, flex my muscles, and get into fighting stance. "No," I reply. "Manywounds is what I'm going to give you."

The timing buzzer goes off and we clinch, each trying to get a better hold. Adam has his hand on my shoulder, the other gripping my opposite arm. I'm positioned pretty much the same way, the mats of the dojo squishing beneath our feet. Stepping forward, behind his foot, I pull his arm up over my head and push on his shoulder, knocking him off balance and throwing him to the ground. Sprawling beside him, legs out, my chest tight on his, I slide my arm under his head and grip his gi. Then I lift my leg up for the mount, using my other hand to tighten the lock on his neck, choking him. Adam taps out.

I hop off, put out my hand to help him up, and we set up again. He steps behind me with one foot, grips my gi and belt, and trips me. I fall backwards, slamming into the mat, the air knocked out of my lungs in a grunt. Adam attempts a sloppy mount. I shove my foot into his gut, push him off, and try for the mount myself. We grapple, neither of us getting the advantage, until Adam finally takes my back and slips his sweaty arm under my chin and around my neck for a rear naked choke. This time, I'm the one tapping out. The timer buzzes.

We're both panting and smiling as we come to a stand. "Blake, you're a dirty fighter," I say, slapping him on the shoulder.

"Manywounds, you have a terrible name for jiu-jitsu."

We both move to the side to get a drink of water while the next match goes on. It's fairly even and they both make it the full three minutes. As we're called to line up, the door to the studio opens and Miranda Blake, Adam's twin sister and my more or less girlfriend, walks in. She gives me a little wave and I trip on the edge of the mat.

"If I knew that's all it took to get you to fall, I'd have told her to come by earlier," Adam jokes.

We line up, listen to the latest info on the tournament at the end of May, and bow off the mats. Miranda steps up to meet me.

"Hi Cody." She smiles, her brown hair half-covering her bright hazel eyes.

"How's it going?" I ask, trying to be all cool. I

wrap my arm around her waist and squeeze her in close. She smells sweet and light, like lilacs.

"Eww. Sweat." She giggles and pulls away.

"I thought you liked me sweaty," I tease.

"Hey, I have my dad's SUV tonight. Want a ride home?" She gives me a sly smile.

"Uh . . ." I look over at Adam, who's talking to a few of the guys from class. "What about your brother?"

"He rode his bike. You don't think I'd get the car if he needed a ride too, do you?"

I flash a big grin. "Okay, let me get changed."

A half-hour later we're pulling into the deserted parking lot of the Bow Waters Canoe Club. Outside, the air is warm and fragrant with tiny new leaves and thawing soil opening up on the edges of dirty snow banks. The smell sneaks in to mingle with the polished leather seats of the SUV. Spring is finally here, and the greyness of the trees is slowly giving way to a hazy green. It's still light out, even though it's getting close to eight o'clock. Miranda turns off the engine.

"You don't have to be home right away, do you?" she asks.

I think of my mom. She's probably playing cards with my aunts. I don't need to walk in on that. Besides, she's not too picky about when I get home, as long as I make it in one piece. "Nah, I'm good."

"Cool. Want to watch a movie or something?"

"A movie? I guess."

Miranda squeezes through the front seats and pulls out her laptop. She boots it up as I follow her. The back seats have already been folded down and pillows and blankets make a comfy bed. The computer plays a chick flick, which has people I recognize but no plot I care about. Something about weddings and dresses, I think. I'm not even sure why they make these movies. I mean, if something doesn't blow up, what's the point? I lie back on the pillows. Miranda slides into my arms. My heart races, but I try to act like I get girls all the time. Really, that's not even close to the truth. I'm no virgin, but I don't exactly get swarmed either.

Miranda and I started hanging out a couple of months ago. It began with going to see a movie with her and Adam, then going out for coffee after jiu-jitsu class. That evolved into her driving me home, where we'd stop briefly to feel each other up — but it always stopped there. Just clothes-on touching and once, a breast. That was a good day. But this, with the ready-made bed, this is new. She's a lot bolder this time. I like it. Especially since, in my experience, I'm not the kind of guy girls like her are usually attracted to.

I'm Native — from the Tsuu T'ina nation to be exact — though we live in Calgary and not on the reserve. At school, I get nothing but grief. Yeah, there is an anti-bullying policy, but that seems to only work on paper. I get called names like chief, spear-chucker, or injun, and if I skip a day of school, the teachers think it's because I've been drinking and not because I've had a cold.

It's true I got into some bad trouble about a year and a half ago with my two best friends, Silas and Jarrod. The police and social services were involved. Things got pretty grim. Silas got juvenile detention. Jarrod and I were assigned community service. My mom called the elders of our family and they had a meeting about me. Uncle Tom came by to talk. He suggested I find something to take up my extra energy. I picked jiu-jitsu. We are a nation of warriors after all, and mixed martial arts is cool.

These days, I only see Jarrod when he bothers to show up at school. I don't go over to his house much anymore. Silas hangs out there, and he still blames me for being thrown in jail. I run into him at school once in a while too. He usually ignores me or flips me the finger from afar. It's his tricks that are my main problem. This year alone, he's packed my locker with snow *three times*, and last December he gave out my e-mail to every spammer in the world. I used to get sixty messages a day about cheap Viagra until I changed my e-mail address. Lately he's been smiling at me in the hallway. I'm not sure if he's up to something or he's noticed how buff I've become and is scared to mess with me now.

Nah, he must be planning something.

The girls have been noticing my muscles lately too. They've been asking me to help them lift stuff and talking me up around my locker. I think it's because I went from a six-foot-two shoestring to a six-foot-two chiselled god. I'm not really that full of myself, but man, working out is good for the abs and the social status. I'd never date those two-faced dye-jobs who called me names a year ago, but it's still flattering.

Miranda is different from the girls in my school. She has dark hair and perfect teeth. She's never even mentioned my race or treated me like anything other than me. I like that. I try not to let things like Native/non-Native bug me. But it's always there. Always hanging over me and my friends. I'm proud of who I am. My people were here long before all the losers who try to push me around.

Miranda nestles her head against my chest as someone on the screen spins and laughs, flower petals flying. I'm really not following this plot. It doesn't seem like she is either. Her fingers move up and under my shirt, feeling my stomach. I tense my muscles, trying to make them seem more ripped.

"Can I see?" Miranda asks with a devilish grin.

I lift my Tapout shirt to show my washboard abs. She runs her fingertips over them. I have to work hard not to squirm, it tickles so badly. But cool guys do not squirm. Or giggle. And I'm really trying to be cool.

"You're so sexy," she says.

Blood courses through every part of my body,

pounding my veins like a punching bag. I'm about to combust. I decide to go for it. "Your turn. Let me see."

Steeling myself for a smack across the face, I'm happy when instead Miranda grabs the bottom of her t-shirt and lifts it to reveal her lacy bra. I dart a look through the window. The parking lot is still empty. I run my fingers over her belly button ring, its diamond glinting in the yellow-orange of sunset, then continue to the top button of her jeans. Stop. Look up. I try to keep my eyes kind of unfocused and hazy, like the guys on reality shows do when they're coming on to a girl.

"Are you going to be sick?" she asks.

"Uh . . ." I stammer, refocusing my eyes. "No, I'm fine." So much for TV as sex ed. "Do you want to . . . you know —"

"Make out?" Miranda finishes for me. "Oh yeah."

We kiss for a while, Miranda's fingers undoing the button of my jeans and loosening the zipper. After that, things move pretty fast. We're both naked and breathing hard.

"We have to stop," Miranda pants, "unless you have something."

"Hang on." I fish around in the mound of clothes and find my jeans. In the back pocket is my wallet. Inside is the condom my sister, Stella, put in my Christmas stocking as a joke. Mom didn't think it was that funny. But like Stella said, I was going to be doing it eventually and I may as well be prepared. I'm glad for her sisterly concern. She must have known I used my last condom right before Carly Yellow Horse's dad chased me across the field at the Christmas Powwow.

I hold up the flat package. "I have protection." It's been in my wallet ever since I got it. I thought it would make me look hot. Available. A player. No one really noticed, but I'm glad I have it on me now. I fumble with the package and Miranda slips it on for me. Then I'm inside her and things are feeling so, so good. Our skin is golden in the sunlight. The SUV is rocking and our breath is starting to steam up the windows as the temperature outside begins to drop. Things go pretty smoothly until I get a leg cramp and Miranda, moving to see what made me stop, hits her head on the back door. Kicking my leg out to uncramp it, I knock the computer over and Miranda scrambles out from under me to make sure it's all right. At last, we get back to our former position — her underneath me, my hips pumping hard. Finally, we're both there and I can't hold back anymore. I let out a groan. It's amazing. My breathing slows and I go to pull out, when a loud knock on the SUV's window makes us both jump.

Chapter 2

I roll off Miranda and onto my stomach, darting my eyes to the source of the sound. It's the cops, their two big faces barely visible through the steamed-up windows.

"Hi there!" one of them booms. "Care to step out of the vehicle?"

We both scramble around each other, trying to find our clothes and turn them the right way out. Miranda fumbles with her bra while I struggle to put on my ginch and jeans while sitting. Not easy. I have them up and over my hips before I remember I still have a fully loaded condom hanging off my quickly deflating wiener. I'm about to reach into my pants and yank it off when the officer thumps once more on the window.

"Hurry up in there," he bellows.

What a dick.

I decide to leave the condom and take care of

it later. It will probably just fall off anyway. Finally dressed, I pull on my shoes and climb out the back door. The biggest cop stands there looking serious and intimidating. The younger one tries to look bad-ass as well, but I catch him smirking when he thinks I'm looking at the ground in shame. I'm not ashamed. I just got laid. Things are pretty damn good.

Miranda finally climbs out too and stands beside me. The younger cop is sent off to run the plates and our IDs. They must figure I stole the vehicle or something. Racial profiling rears its ugly head again.

"You know, what you were doing was illegal," Mr. Tough Cop says, giving me a stern look.

"Sex is illegal?" I say. I know what he's getting at, but I don't want to play along. This guy just wants to intimidate me. I won't be intimidated by cops. Ever.

"Sex in public is. We could give you a fine. Take the car. Call your parents." The cop ticks off these possibilities on his sausage fingers.

Miranda goes pale. "Please," she whispers. "Don't call my —"

"No one was around," I say, pointing to the empty parking lot, "except you guys." I lean forward and narrow my eyes. "So, how long were you watching? Huh? Get a good show?"

Miranda goes so white she's almost transparent. "Cody, cut it out," she hisses.

Mr. Tough Cop clears his throat. "Who owns the vehicle?"

"My dad," Miranda whispers.

"Does he know you have it out?" he asks.

She nods.

"I'll bet he doesn't know what you've been doing in it, huh?"

She shakes her head and stares at her shoes. Tears trickle down her cheeks, painting them black with streaks of mascara. It pisses me off, the way the cop is laying into her like that. So we were screwing. So what? Like he never did that in his life.

"Why don't you just leave her alone, you piece of —"

"The vehicle's clean and so are they," the younger cop says, saving me from saying something I'd probably regret. "He has a record." The cop nods toward me. "But nothing outstanding."

Mr. Tough Cop gives me a hard look, like he's just waiting for me to jump on him or blow up in his face. Waiting for me to give him a reason to arrest me that won't make him look like a jerk. Finally he says, "I'll let you two off with a warning this time. But don't let me catch you back here again. This is a public area. If you want to have sexual relations, have them at your homes. And if you can't," he sets his gaze on Miranda, "then you probably shouldn't be having them in your dad's SUV either. Understand?"

"Thank you," Miranda whispers, wiping her cheeks with the back of her hand. "We won't do it again."

"Ever again, probably," I mutter, thinking of how the cop just let it slip that I have a nasty past.

We get into the SUV and Miranda pulls out of the parking lot, the cops following us for a while in their car. The tip of my dick is starting to feel a bit on the cold and soggy side, and my underwear is damp, like I forgot to shake after taking a whizz.

We drive in silence for a while. Miranda misses the turnoff to my street and has to backtrack. I figure I need to break this funk she's in. I put on Mr. Tough Cop's voice and wag my finger. "Having fun is illegal. Breathing? That's illegal. And damn it, being a teenager is illegal. You are very, very bad. But I am a nice cop, I'll let you go — for now! But if I catch you again, I'm going to video-tape it and post it on YouTube."

Miranda stops sniffling and gives me a little smile.

"That's better," I tell her.

"I was so worried," she says. "If they called my dad . . . I don't even want to think about what would happen."

"Nah." I dismiss this with a swipe of my hand. "They were never going to do that. That guy was just in it for the power trip. Protecting the peace, my ass!"

"Still, I'm glad they didn't." She drives in silence once more, finally pulling up in front of my house. "Cody —"

"Miranda," I reply, matching her tone.

"Stop it," she laughs, swatting me. "Is it true

what he said? That you have a criminal record?"

I take a deep breath. I was hoping she would just pretend that didn't happen. "I guess," I say, deciding to amend the truth. I don't really want to get into it with her just now, so I invent a story. "I got caught shoplifting when I was twelve."

"Shoplifting what?" she asks, looking pretty relieved.

"Nothing much. Just a hamster."

"You tried to shoplift a hamster?" Miranda starts cracking up, letting out all the built-up fear and tension from our interrupted date.

"Yeah. Do you know how hard it is to hide a hamster down your pants?"

She swats me again, laughing. "Cody, you're a real nut job."

"You know it." I give her a kiss on the cheek and push open the door to the SUV. "See you on Saturday."

As I step out onto the curb and turn to close the door, Miranda points and giggles. "Are you sure you weren't scared of those cops?"

I raise my eyebrow. "Huh?"

She points at my crotch. "You look like you peed yourself."

On the front of my jeans, the denim is a dark, wet blue. "The condom," I explain. "Must have finally slipped off."

"Sure," she winks. "Or maybe you have another hamster down there."

"Ooh, you are kinky," I reply as I shut the door.

After Miranda drives away, I head up to the house. Mom waves through a gap in the curtains, her long black hair swept over her shoulder, her eyes smiling. She's sitting at the dining room table with four of my aunts and my cousin Jennie, drinking tea and playing cards. My good mood drops like a man at the end of his rope. It feels like I'm on some kind of sadistic emotional roller coaster. One minute I'm happy, then I'm in ecstasy, then embarrassed, followed by annoyed, then mad, then happy again, ending with . . . depressed. Yeah, depressed is the emotion I'll go with here. I know if Jennie's around, I'm going to get hassled. I rub my hand over my bristly hair and pull open the front door to our house.

Chapter 3

"Cody!" Mom announces, like she's some kind of game show host. My cousin Jennie giggles and my aunts laugh, waving their cards at me. I pull my jiu-jitsu bag strategically in front of my damp crotch.

"So, what were you up to?" Jennie asks, winking cheekily. She clasps her fingers, hoping for some spicy news.

Miranda naked, our gasping sighs, and the cops banging on the window all flash through my head. "I was at practice," I say. I've learned that telling the truth never works — especially with Jennie. It just leads to gossip and teasing, and she's an expert at that. I don't need that kind of hassle right now. Actually, I don't need that kind of hassle *ever*.

Jennie shakes her head and chuckles. "Practice, huh? Sure you were."

"I was," I frown. Jennie is so annoying. Flicking her hair, her eyes all wide looking for any telltale cringe that would let her know she's on the right track.

"Come on. Your class ended at least an hour ago."

"I went to Tim Hortons after with Adam Blake and his sister," I explain.

Jennie shakes her head, not believing a word. "So who dropped you off?"

"Like I said, Adam and Miranda."

"I only saw one person in the van, and it wasn't a boy."

"Adam was in the back seat," I say, not even flinching. "Didn't you see him? Maybe you're going blind." I shake my head, knowing I'm treading on some pretty thin ground. If one of my aunts or my mom noticed that no one else was in the SUV, I'm busted. But it's worth a try. I mean, prisoners get grilled less than I do. All I want to do is get to my room, take off my wet pants, lie down, and shut off. Maybe even study for my Bio test. But getting away from Jennie is never that easy. She'll just follow me.

"So, Cody," one of my aunts says, "your mom was telling us you'll be done high school in a few months. Are you going to work with your Uncle Tom?"

I shrug. "Maybe for the summer. I'm hoping to go to university in September."

"Why would you want to go to university?" Jennie sneers. "You'll be lucky to graduate high school."

"I get pretty good marks," I say, sneering back.

"I have honours in Biology."

"Biology, huh? What do you want to be, a doctor?" She flips her hair again. "Doctor Many-wounds. That sounds so wrong."

I want to punch her, but my aunts wouldn't put up with that and Jennie knows it. She's the youngest of us cousins, born three weeks after me. With no other grandkids living close enough to take her place yet, she's still the baby of the family. But I'll get her later. Put salt in her tea or something. "I'm not planning on being a doctor," I say. "I'm going to be an MMA fighter."

"Right, because mixed martial arts is something you can take in university."

I huff. "You're so stupid."

The aunts *ooh* and giggle, loving the entertainment.

"I'm going to take physiotherapy or sports medicine," I explain.

"You should get a real job. Doctors don't actually work. They never have calluses, just loads and loads of pills," Jennie says.

"I'm not going to be a doctor," I repeat.

"My brother went to university and you know what happened to him," she states. "It will happen to you too, just watch."

"Shut up!" I snap.

Jennie juts her chin out. "Make me."

"Oh, leave the boy alone, Jennie," Mom finally says. "He's tired, and who cares if he wants to go to university. It's his decision."

But Jennie won't quit. I've been her living chew toy since we were young. "I know why you want to go, Cody — you *love* to hook up with the girls, don't you?"

I decide to play along and see if that will give me a ticket to freedom. I cross my heart with my finger and give Jennie my most angelic smile. "Girls? I would *never*. I'm as clean as the freshly fallen snow."

Mom and all my aunts fall on each other with laughter, wiping their eyes and gasping.

"Oh yeah?" Jennie taunts. "Tell that to Carly Yellow Horse's dad."

"I did," I reply. "But I don't think he believed me."

"I wonder why," Jennie says, giggling. "You were just lucky he caught you while you still had your underwear on. No one needed to see your naked butt."

Carly Yellow Horse. The mention of that night forces blood to rush to my face, and a few other places. I make sure my bag is still firmly in front of my crotch. It's a good thing all the grown-ups believed the story Carly and I fed them — that her dad caught us as we were taking our clothes off, not just as we were putting them back on.

"Like I said, I'm as clean as the fallen snow." I glance at the pile of mail on the counter. Just bills and junk from what I can see. I'm waiting for a letter, but it doesn't look like it's here yet. "Anyway, I have to study. I have a test in Biology tomorrow. So if you'll excuse me . . ."

"Just quit while you're ahead," Jennie says, still laughing. But I can tell I'm pretty much done as a topic of interest. Already the aunts have started talking about the ladies they saw at bingo two days ago, and Jennie is wondering out loud where Uncle Tom got the money for his new truck.

I go down the hall to my room. Once my door is closed, I quickly take off my soggy jeans and underwear. The condom still clings to my shrivelled dick. It has an inch-long tear at the tip. That must be why my pants got so wet. I guess they weren't made to be worn for a half an hour after sex. Who knew? There goes the next big fashion trend.

I yank the condom off, wrap it in a tissue, and shove it to the bottom of my garbage can on the off chance that Jennie decides to go through my trash. I wouldn't put it past her. Grabbing clean pants and ginch, I get re-dressed. There's a knock on my bedroom door just as I pull up my zipper. "Cody," Mom calls. "I'm driving your aunts home. Jennie's coming too. Your sister will be home in a minute. Keep an eye on things for me, eh?"

I let out a happy sigh. It's been hell since Jennie moved in a year ago, after her brother died and her mom got depressed and ended up in the hospital. I'm grateful for any time without that she-devil around. As the door to the house slams shut, I sit down at my desk and turn on my computer. I should boot up my notes for the Bio test, try to study my unit on reproduction and development, but instead I open Facebook. Miranda has just posted: *Cops caught me and my boyfriend doing the nasty! LOL.*

Great! I think. *Now Adam is going to beat me up for real.* He's only sort of okay with me seeing his twin sister. I doubt he'll be fine with me having sex with her. I wonder how often he checks the news feed.

I click over to the University of Toronto's page. It's the university I most want to go to. I've put in an application to the University of Calgary too, mainly because my family wants me to stick close and my Uncle Tom can give me a job in the summers. But really, I just want to get away. Get out on my own. My family is there for me, but they also kind of hold me back. No one really thinks I'm going to make it out of high school and most of them don't get why I want to bother with university. Some of them, like Jennie, just out-and-out put me down for trying in the first place. Silas calls me an apple. You know, red on the outside, white on the inside. But what does he know? His whole goal in life is to cause mischief and not get caught. Some career. Jarrod isn't much better. He could do so much more with his life than work in his dad's auto body shop. He's smart enough, and a really good artist. But he has no ambition. He's happy to putter around airbrushing things instead of going to SAIT so he can get his ticket and make the big bucks. I'm more realistic. I know that MMA probably isn't going to pay the bills. I figure physiotherapy might be a good way to stay in the sport and make a living. Besides, university is filled with hot chicks and I'm all about that. Cute girls, parties, and clubs. The U of T has over eight hundred clubs and a place called Aboriginal House, so I can stay connected with my culture. They probably have cute girls there too.

The only thing that kind of sucks is I'm going to have to break it off with Miranda in a couple of months. She has a sports scholarship to the University of Alberta in Edmonton. We haven't really talked about it, but I think she probably knows it too. It's too bad, because after this afternoon's action, things have gotten interesting. We could probably keep in touch on Skype or something, but I don't really want a long-distance relationship. I'd rather be single next year and keep myself open to all opportunities.

The front door opens with a squeak, then slams shut. Footsteps click in the hall.

"Hey Cody," Stella says, knocking and opening my bedroom door at once.

Seriously, I have absolutely no privacy in this house.

"I have something for you," she grins.

"What?" I ask her. "Poison for Jennie?"

"Cody!" Stella slaps my arm with a thin, padded package before putting it on my dresser. "Was Jennie bugging you again?"

"She's such a pain. She was going after me

about messing around with girls, just because I was late getting home. She makes me sound like such a perv."

Stella looks at me, a slow smile creeping over her face. "So were you . . .?" She makes humping motions with her hands.

"Jeez, you too?" But I can't help grinning. "Yeah," I admit. "I was. But we kind of got interrupted."

"Again?"

"By the cops this time." I put on my best scowl to counter her extreme glee. "Really, it's not that funny."

"Little brother, it is hilarious."

"Glad you think so."

Stella sits down on my bed. "So, who was it? Carly Yellow Horse?"

"What? No!"

"Then who?"

"You wouldn't know her."

"Someone from school?"

"No. Adam Blake's sister, Miranda."

Stella puts her hand in front of her mouth to cover her laugh. "Your training partner's twin sister?"

"And she posted it on Facebook," I add.

Stella howls with laughter. "Cody, you are in deep trouble."

I pull my hand over my short hair and groan. "I know. I'm dead."

"I'll say something nice at your funeral."

"I feel like an idiot."

"You are an idiot. You should never go out with the sister of someone you already fight. Is he better than you?"

I think about it. "A little, but we're pretty even."

The front door slams and I hear Mom and Jennie head to the kitchen with a yell of, "We're back!"

"Don't say anything to them," I plead. "Please. I'll never hear the end of it."

"I've got your back," she says, with a wink. Stella stands up. "By the way, Dad finally sent us Christmas presents." She grabs the small padded envelope she put on my dresser. "Here. I'm assuming it's a crappy CD. He got me Justin Bieber. Like I'm seven or something," she scoffs.

I open the package. It's a Johnny Cash CD. Nothing against the guy, but I prefer Winnipeg's Most, Plex, and Lil Wayne. "Jarrod will love this."

"Is he still listening to those old country guys?"

"Just like his dad." I put the CD on my desk. "I'll take it to his house if he isn't at school tomorrow."

"Silas might get you if you go over there," Stella warns.

I think of the cops, Miranda, and her Facebook post. "Not if Adam gets me first."

Chapter 4

"You had sex with my sister? Now you must die!" Adam's voice bellows as he pulls a razor-sharp samurai sword from his belt. I wake up damp and tangled for at least the seventh time. The first six dreams featured lightsabers, M16's, and, the nightmare before this, a grenade. I decide to get up, have a shower, and make some coffee. I guess I fear Adam more than I thought. Probably because the next time I'll see him is this Saturday, when we have mixed martial arts together. It's a class where we're encouraged to beat the crap out of each other. I'm so doomed.

"You're up early," Mom says, coming into the kitchen just as the coffee begins to trickle into the pot. She stands by the counter, impatiently holding a cup and popping some bread into the toaster. She's still in her big, bulky bathrobe and wearing furry black moccasins that my grandma beaded.

Her long hair is tangled and she looks pretty sleepy. She doesn't start her job at the bookstore until nine. Mornings around here move pretty slowly.

"I have a test today. I thought I'd get some more studying in."

"You sure work hard," she smiles.

With toast on her plate and coffee in her cup, Mom comes to sit beside me. She rubs my head, the smell of sweet grass smudge coming off of her. "You're doing good, Cody. You've really straightened out since you were fifteen. I'm proud of you. I doubt you'll find half as much trouble as I did at your age."

I know Mom is hoping I don't end up like her — sixteen, pregnant, and married to a guy who never really stuck around. (I haven't told her yet, but boys can't get pregnant and I don't plan on marrying a dude.) I know she cares. She doesn't say as much, but I can feel it. That's why she calls our elders when Stella or I have trouble. She wants us to know what's right and what's wrong, or at least have the chance to find out on our own.

"I don't know about that," I say to her. "I seem to be good at finding trouble."

It's going to be difficult to hook up with Miranda again now that Adam knows I've been playing Doctor Manywounds with his sister. I wonder if he holds back when he's fighting me at the dojo. We might not be as evenly matched as I think.

"I'm going to school," I say, getting up.

"An hour early?" Mom asks, surprised. "Are you meeting up with Jarrod and Silas?"

"Nah, Jarrod won't be around this early and Silas still won't talk to me — but at least he hasn't pulled a prank on me in a while, so that's something." I push my chair in. "The library is open and I forgot my text book in my locker," I lie. Really, I just want to get out of the house and away from thoughts of Adam kicking the crap out of me.

From coffee with Mom to the blur of Bio class, my morning is a mess. All I can see during the whole test is me in a choke hold, and Adam not letting go. Later, in Math, I can't do even the most basic addition: one fist plus one eye makes me blind. By lunchtime, I'm a bit of a mess.

"Chief! Chief!" The voice calls through the masses and down the hall, where I'm walking aimlessly, trying to convince my stomach to accept a ham sandwich. It's not working. A hand falls on my shoulder and a big blond guy in a basketball uniform, who looks like he could be a stand-in for Thor, spins me to face him. "I said, Chief."

I scowl and toss the sandwich into the nearby trash can. "I'm not the chief of anything," I reply, "but thanks for the promotion." I go to turn away.

"Sorry, I don't know your name," the kid says, not letting go of my shoulder.

"Cody. Yours?" I stick out my hand and the kid finally releases his grip. He doesn't shake though.

"Harek."

"Hi Harek. I'm assuming you aren't here to ask for an autograph. So, what do you want?" I sound a lot more confident than I feel. The guy isn't taller than me. If anything, I may be taller than him. After a year of martial arts, I might be stronger too. Still, I get the distinct feeling he doesn't respect me. Might be the whole Chief thing, but who knows.

Harek leans in close and lowers his voice. "The deal is, Chief, I'm looking for someone who can supply some booze and pot for my party tonight. Word is you might be the guy to talk to."

I shake my head. Even at my absolute worst, I never ran drugs or alcohol. I know where to draw the line. I do actually *want* to get into university, as weird as that sounds. "Who told you that?"

Harek points down the hall. Silas waves and gives me a grin before running off. I turn back to the would-be party animal. "Sorry, I can't help you."

"Come on," Harek whines. "Don't be a dick. Seriously, I can pay you. You need the money, don't you?"

I frown. "Why?"

"Why what?"

"Why do you think I need the money?" Now I'm getting paranoid. In the back of my mind — the totally unreasonable, jump-to-conclusions part of my brain — I'm thinking he knows I have a crazy-mad martial artist after me and I need a bodyguard. Or years of physical therapy. Or a full-time nurse — yeah, a full-time nurse, that would be awesome. Then my brain snaps back to reality and I feel like a totally hysterical freak.

"Aren't you broke all the time?" Harek says. "You're Native, right?"

I nod. "Yes, very Native, thanks for noticing."

"So you can get me hooked up with booze, right?"

"Umm," I say, shaking my head. "I hate to break it to you, but just because I'm Native doesn't mean they open the liquor stores and look the other way when I tell them I'm underage."

"But don't you guys —"

"What guys?" I interrupt. "Being Native isn't like some kind of boy scout club. There isn't a beer-running badge or anything." I turn away from him and start to walk down the hall, waving over my shoulder. "You'll have to find your booze somewhere else."

I know it's coming — I see it out of the corner of my eye. Not only is Harek a racist, he's a coward. The punch almost lands on the back of my head before I spin, catch his fist, and bend his wrist at entirely the wrong angle. He's on the floor looking up at me, his eyes begging me not to break bones. "Leave me alone," I mutter, before letting him go. I move off down the hall just as Mr. Flemming, our principal, comes around the corner.

"Dirty Indian!" Harek yells.

Mr. Flemming either doesn't hear the insult or

doesn't care. He continues on and disappears into the mass of students.

"What did you say?" I ask, heading back.

"You heard me," Harek says, looking like he has just realized he may have made a big mistake.

I grab the front of his shirt and throw a punch at his head, stopping millimetres from his nose. "Don't ever call me, or anyone else, that again. If you do, I'll mess up that stupid, white face of yours so bad you'll be breathing out your ass." I let him go and he scampers off, his ears red.

There's a group of kids starting to gather and the principal isn't far away. I know I'll be the one that's blamed if Harek says anything. Deciding to make myself scarce, I head to the auto body classroom and see if Jarrod, my only real friend, is hanging out there. When he's at school, he usually spends his lunch hour welding panels, fixing dents, and painting flames on cars that have no business having flames. Today, he's not around.

"Hey Cody." Mr. Greene greets me with a wave. "Where's your buddy?"

"I was looking for him too."

"I have a great opportunity for him, but I need to talk to him first."

So Jarrod is skipping again. That isn't too surprising. He gets in the zone in his dad's garage, fixing classic cars, and sometimes loses track of time. If he wasn't so talented, Mr. Greene would have had him suspended ages ago. He's constantly going to bat for Jarrod.

Jarrod's been helping out in his dad's shop since he could carry a wrench in one hand and a bottle in the other. After his mom died five years ago, from complications with her diabetes, he and his dad got even closer. His dad's not one to get upset if Jarrod doesn't go to school, or even if he has a beer or two. He's not that kind of parent. He just wants Jarrod to be happy. To do whatever it is he feels like doing. He told me once that he thought Jarrod would find his own road eventually and the fastest way for him to do it was if everyone just got out of the way.

After mandatory attendance in two blurry afternoon classes, where I sat doodling and not keeping my mind on Hamlet or much else, the end-of-school bell finally rings. I head to my locker to grab my jacket and throw my homework into my backpack.

Silas races past, chased by a bunch of grade ten boys in shorts and t-shirts. He flashes his trademark grin and waves. "I think I may have gone too far this time," he calls.

The guys behind him are trailing thick, foamy bubbles from their shoes and legs. And they look angry. Really, really angry. I follow the trail of bubbles back to its source, the boys' locker room. Opening the door, I let loose a tidal wave of foam, almost up to my hips. The smell of lemony dish soap fills the air and makes me choke. The sound of squeaking bucket wheels being rushed frantically down the hall sends me and my pants, now squelching, speed walking toward the main doors. I don't need to be caught in the middle of this, but it is pretty damn funny.

"Check the library. I think he ran that way," I tell a confused grade ten boy who zips by me. They won't find Silas. He's really good at disappearing. My grandma used to call him Dik'oyi when he was young — Coyote. But that was before he went away to Saskatchewan with his mom and her new boyfriend. When Silas came back, he was different. More serious. He didn't really talk about what had gone on there or why he had hitchhiked back on his own to live with his uncle.

All we knew was that things had changed. Silas started making friends with some pretty sketchy marijuana growers. He got involved in stealing, selling pot, stuff like that. Jarrod and I told him what he was doing was a bad idea, but then he began buying us new skateboards, loads of spray paint, and all the junk food we could eat. Every weekend we would go skating and tagging, smoke dope, and have a few beers. It started small, but by the end we were all into joyriding, picking up girls, and acting cool. For a bunch of fifteen-year-olds, life was pretty awesome.

Then, in one stupid night, things went bad. Really bad. Silas had to deliver a block of hash to this guy who scared the crap out of him, so he asked Jarrod and I to come along. We agreed, but we weren't too happy about it. Still, it was fun just skating and shooting the breeze. Suddenly, Silas stopped outside this plain blue house.

"I know the guy that lives here," he said. "He's a total moron."

It turned out the kid who lived there had been bugging Silas for a while. He was gone, on holiday to Florida or something, so we decided we were going to give the kid some payback. It took about two seconds for Silas to crack the lock and get us in. We found the kid's room pretty fast.

"Let's mess it up!" Silas declared.

So we ripped the room apart. Cut up the mattress, trashed the trophies and the dresser. Just destroyed the place. It was pretty fun, wrecking stuff and not even thinking of the outcome. Silas decided we should take the kid's computer and sell it. He was just untangling all the wires when I heard a noise. Jarrod and I took off right away, running straight into the arms of the cops outside. Silas was still in the kid's bedroom holding the computer with a backpack full of hash and dope when they got to him.

Cuffed and sitting on the curb, Jarrod and I were freaking out and bawling so much the cops couldn't even understand our answers to their questions. Silas, though, was calm as anything. He told the cops that he had found the drugs in the house, in the mattress we had sliced up. Jarrod and I went along with this story accidentally by being frantic and useless. A few hours after we got to the police station, my mom and Jarrod's dad came to bail the two of us out. No one came for Silas.

Uncle Tom came over the next day, took me for a hike, and told me some stories from his childhood and a couple of legends from our people. He never said what I did was wrong, or even made much in the way of suggestions. He only told me I might want to look into a better hobby than drinking and stealing cars, and that following a trickster was good way to get into trouble. In the end, he left it up to me to find the right way. When the police stopped by the next day to ask more questions, I decided to admit that the drugs hadn't been in the house. I think they already knew that. They didn't seem overly surprised. I didn't say anything else about where they had come from, just that they hadn't come from there. Silas still thought I was the one who ratted him out. Maybe I did. But it still felt like the right thing to do. I mean, the kid whose house we trashed might have been a jerk, but we weren't much better.

I push open the front doors of the school and step outside. Silas comes tearing out behind me, laughing. The grade ten boys are nowhere in sight.

Chapter 5

"Dik'oyi gets away again," I say, half expecting Silas to turn around and punch me in the head.

"Every time," Silas replies, stopping, a grin taking up most of his face. "No one can catch a coyote."

"That was a great prank," I admit.

"So you saw it, huh?"

"Stood in it, actually."

Silas looks down at my foamy, damp pants and laughs some more. Silas is as plump and round as Jarrod is thin and angular. I don't mean he's fat. Not at all. He actually reminds me of a puppy, with his wide face, sandy brown hair, and the way he always seems to be moving even when he's standing still.

"I've never seen so many bubbles. How'd you do it?" I ask as we start walking away from the school.

"I found some dry ice lying around," Silas says.

"'Found' as in . . ."

"Maybe lifted," he admits. "It was in the chemistry lab. I'm not sure why it was there, but it gave me this idea. I heard if you put dry ice in a bucket of warm water with a whole bottle of dish detergent, you get loads of bubbles."

"So you thought you'd try it out."

"And give the grade ten gym class a treat. I mean, they're forced to take gym, so why not show them we care about their pain and suffering?"

"Gym isn't painful," I say.

"Speak for yourself." Silas laughs again. "So how high did it get?"

"It was up to my waist when I went in."

Silas pumps his fist in the air and lets out a whoop. "Man, Cody, I haven't talked to you in ages. I get all my news from Jarrod and he hardly sees you either."

"I thought you were still mad about . . . you know."

"Me?" Silas lets out a yip. "That's old news. I've been over it for ages."

"Yeah, right! You filled my locker with snow three times! I had to shut down my e-mail account and get a new one because I got so much Viagra spam, and every time I saw you, you gave me the finger. Then there was that Viking basketball player you set on me at lunch."

Silas laughs. "Oh, that. That was just a joke."

"Some joke," I sneer. "I had to put the guy in a

41

jiu-jitsu move to get him to leave me alone."

Silas laughs even more, snorting and hiccuping in the process. "That's funny. Okay, maybe I was still a bit mad, but you've suffered enough and I miss the three of us hanging out together. Jarrod's okay on his own, but he doesn't like to do much except work on cars and hang out at his house. You should come by more often. I mean, I was thinking —"

"I thought I smelled smoke," I joke.

"Funny," Silas says, pointing his fingers at me like a gunslinger. "We're both almost eighteen."

"Yeah, and . . ."

"We're going to have to live our own lives soon."

I think of Silas living his own life since he was born. So different from me, with my extended family of aunts, cousins, and grandparents who are just a phone call away.

"I think we should get our old crew back together. Me, you, and Jarrod."

"And you try to tell me this by stuffing my locker full of snow?" I ask.

Silas laughs again before something catches his attention. "Yo, baby!" he yells, whistling.

A group of university girls are protesting a half a block away, chanting "Our bodies, our choice." Silas looks at me and we both break into wolfish grins. Then, without a word, we cross the street to support their cause. Hey, anything to do with girls and their bodies, I'm there.

I zero in on a long-haired girl with a sign, but before I can reach her, a grizzled old hippy steps in front of me and shoves a pamphlet in my hand. Cops and TV crews pull up and start interviewing anyone they can talk to. Silas and I know it's time to get out of there. I stuff the pamphlet into my backpack without even looking at it and dart one last glance at the girl.

Silas and I slip past an old Chinese guy and a plump girl I recognize from school, and turn down Seventeenth Avenue. The air is dusty and the cars are loud. I have to raise my voice to be heard. "So, where are you living now?" I ask, realizing I have over a year to catch up on, now that Silas and I are talking again.

"With my aunt."

"Is she nice?"

He shrugs. "She told me last night that she's kicking me out at the end of June. She figures once I turn eighteen, she's done."

"Crappy," I say.

"Whatever."

"Why don't you go back to your mom?"

Silas narrows his eyes and pulls his arms around him. "Mom made her choice. I'm not going back there."

I feel sorry for him. Silas hasn't had an easy life. His mom has had too many boyfriends, and his dad, a Texan trucker, took off early in his life. Kind of like mine — except his doesn't even send Christmas presents in April. His aunts and uncles view him as shameful and everyone else, like my mom, shares that opinion.

Silas tells me about his life, how he got sent to a group home after jail, how the aunt who got him out freaks if she gets any call from the school — even if it's only about graduation pictures. "I was thinking of opening a restaurant," Silas says. "You know, in a few years or so. I'll call it Coyote Café and put all my favourite recipes on the menu."

I laugh. "Like what? Mac and cheese and peanut butter sandwiches?"

"Ha, ha," he says. "You sound like my aunt."

"I'm just joking." I punch his arm. "I'd come in for a bison burger or two. Where are you going to get the money to do this?"

Silas clicks his tongue. "I have a plan."

We head over to Jarrod's. Sure enough, I find him expertly airbrushing a skull on a black and silver 1970 Chevrolet El Camino in his father's shop. His dad is singing along to George Jones blaring out of the big yellow stereo beside him. The whole place smells of paint fumes, grease, and Varsol. Jarrod's dad looks up, waves, then goes back to sanding a panel of a 1979 T-Bird. Jarrod glances up from his work and his long, thin face breaks in two as a smile cuts across it. He gives the airbrush a quick clean, then, wiping his hands on a rag, walks over to greet us. His long black hair is tinted silver from the paint he was working with, and a metallic orange streak lies across one jutting cheekbone.

"Cody! Silas! What the hell?"

"I know. He's talking to me again," Silas says, grinning. "We're back in action, the three trouble-makers."

"I got something for you." I hand Jarrod the Johnny Cash CD.

He turns it over in his hands. "This is great. Where'd you get it?"

"My dad just sent it for Christmas."

Jarrod lets out a deep throaty laugh. "Well, it's either really late or super early. Tell you what, I'll trade you. Taylor Manyguns just gave me a CD him and his boys made. I didn't want to hurt his feelings, but it sounds like angry squirrels chittering out a Dr. Seuss book." Jarrod gets into his best hip-hop stance and starts barking, "Red fish, blue fish, girl's titties, boobs — I'm Taylor Manyguns and I'm a goof. Yo!" He flashes a gang symbol before resuming his laid-back slouch. "I thought you might like it."

"Uh . . . thanks?" I say. We follow him out across the alley, through the backyard, and into his house. In the kitchen, Jarrod grabs the CD. Taylor has Photoshopped himself with a half-naked girl on the cover, her hands all over him. Like that would ever happen. He looks like the Native version of the Michelin Man.

Jarrod shouts, his head inside the refrigerator. "You guys want a beer?"

"Sure," Silas says. "What's a couple of months, give or take? I'm almost eighteen."

"I better not. Don't need Jennie spreading rumours that I'm a drunk or anything," I answer.

He hands Silas a beer and me a Coke, then grabs another for himself. "You are so whipped."

I sneer. "You try having her for a cousin."

"Want to stay for dinner, Cody?" Jarrod asks, as we head out to his backyard and collapse into stained plastic chairs, resting our feet on the fire-pit. The backyard looks like a car graveyard. "We're having our usual Friday night pizza party. Carly is coming over. She would love to see you." Jarrod winks. "Silas is staying too, right?"

"Like I would miss free food," Silas scoffs.

"Sorry, can't," I say, even though the thought of seeing Carly makes my face go hot. "I have to be up early for martial arts tomorrow. Besides, I think I've had nearly enough of Silas for one day. Do you know what he did at lunch?"

Jarrod grins, glancing at Silas. "What?"

"Set a Viking basketball player on me."

Jarrod chokes on his drink, laughing as I retell the drama. "By the way, Mr. Greene was looking for you," I say.

"Mr. Greene, Mr. Greene . . ." Jarrod says, pointing his nose to the sky.

"Your auto body teacher."

"Yeah, yeah. He's hassling me to do my apprenticeship at a collision repair shop. You know, SUVs and minivans."

"That's what *I've* been telling you. You'd make good money if you got your ticket," I say.

"Ah, not so much. Anyway, I'm happy here with my dad."

"Well, can't you apprentice here?" Silas asks.

"Dad's not a journeyman. He's not official."

I frown. "But don't you *want* to get your ticket?"

Jarrod shrugs. "I can learn the ropes without some piece of paper."

"Yeah," I agree, "but that's not going to fly if you want to work somewhere else."

"Dad never had that kind of stuff. It takes more than formal education to make you a man in this world. I can do all right without it."

"Did you even mention it to your dad?"

"What?" Jarrod scowls. "Did I tell him he isn't a good enough teacher? No." Jarrod takes a long drink from his can and punches me in the arm. "What's been going on? I haven't seen you in ages."

"I got laid last night." It's out of my mouth before I have a chance to think. Mind you, if I had a chance to think, I probably would have said it anyway.

"Who? Carly Yellow Horse?" Silas asks.

"No! What's wrong with you people?"

"Aww, come on. Just because her dad caught you rocking their van and chased you clear across the field with his cane is no reason to break it off with her," Jarrod teases.

"It was never on with her. We just hooked up. That's all."

"That's not what Carly said. Sooo, who is this

girl? Someone I know?"

"Doubt it. She's the twin sister of a guy I work out with at the dojo."

"Holy crap. That's ballsy," Silas yips.

"Yeah, well it was more her idea, and —"

"Yeah? Don't stop." Jarrod leans his face in towards me, grinning ear to ear.

"The cops kind of broke it up."

"Cody, you have the worst luck!" He slaps his knee.

"I know. Just once I want to get laid and not be lectured right afterward."

Jarrod stands up and stretches. "Does her brother know?"

"She posted it on Facebook."

Silas strokes his chin thoughtfully. "He might be illiterate."

"That would be nice."

"When are you seeing her again?" Jarrod asks.

"Right after I see her brother. If I'm still alive."

He smacks me on the back of the head, laughing. "Then you better hope you're still as fast as you were when Carly's dad chased you."

Chapter 6

Miranda and I snuggle in her super-pink bedroom. She was pretty shy about showing me her room the first time, blushing as she explained that the decor was from when she was eight. Honestly, the room could be on fire for all I care. Though the row of My Little Ponies looking at me with their overly big eyes when we're humping kind of creeps me out.

Technically, I'm not allowed into her room. Her family doesn't even know I'm here. I skipped Saturday's MMA class and my two jiu-jitsu classes this week so we could have the house to ourselves while Adam's at the dojo and her parents are still at work. Well, not the MMA class. I skipped that to keep from being killed. Although I'd never admit it to Miranda, I'm still scared of what Adam will do when he finds out we're together.

It's not that her parents don't like me. I've been

over a few times before to hang out with Adam. It's just that Miranda's mom and dad still think she's a virgin. Because of that, she isn't allowed to have boys anywhere near her room. So it's just best if we keep my visits quiet.

Miranda rubs my bare chest with her hand and kisses my skin, giving me goosebumps. "Wouldn't it be funny if we were like this ten years from now?" Miranda says, her voice dreamy.

"What?" I ask, "Still in bed? I think your parents might notice me eventually and get pissed off."

She smacks me, giggling. "You know that's not what I meant. Like, if we were still together."

"That's only going to work if one or both of us gets cloned. You're going to Edmonton in September on a soccer scholarship and I'm not."

"You could go to school there too. Just apply."

I shrug. "I guess. But if we were still together in ten years, we'd have to get married or I'd never hear the end of it from my aunts."

"Miranda Manywounds," she says. "I would sound like the most injured athlete around. You would have to take my name instead."

"Cody Blake?" I ask. "That makes me sound like a private eye." I put on my best fifties gumshoe detective voice and say, "She stood in my office. Tall, dark, and dangerous."

"Oooh, I like where this is going." Miranda grins, kissing me.

"Yeah, and we would be so rich. Both of us

world-class athletes. Me winning big MMA tournaments in the States and you playing on some English soccer team."

"Aww, we would never see each other. That would suck," she pouts.

"We could satisfy ourselves with groupies while we're on the road."

Miranda hits me with a pillow. "Don't you dare, Cody Manywounds. You better stay true to me."

"What? No sex at all for months on end? Seriously?"

"It would make you fight harder."

"It would give me blue balls."

"You're such a baby." Miranda frowns. "So you would be fine with me hanging out with cute English soccer players with blond shaggy hair and sexy accents while you —"

Now I hit her with the pillow. "I said groupies, not fellow athletes. You know, pimple-faced wannabes who are dying to be touched by their hero. Easy, available, but not someone you would want to spend your whole life with."

Miranda shakes her head. "I could never do that to you and you know it. How many kids should we have?"

"Oh," I say, "at least twenty-six."

"Twenty-six!"

"Yeah. Then we can name each one with a different letter in the alphabet. Alexander, Billy, Casper, Doug —"

"Those are all boys."

"Fine. Amy, Bonny, Candice —"

"Why would you want twenty-six, anyway?"

"That's how many I figure it would take to serve my every need. Get the newspaper, make my supper, bring me a beer . . ."

"You're an athlete, remember?"

"Bring me an energy drink . . ."

Miranda shakes her head. "They're children, not slaves." She throws up her hands. "Maybe we shouldn't get married!" she cries out dramatically.

"Man!" I slam my fist on the bed. "Now I'll have to take back all those toasters and corn plates we got for our wedding gifts. This sucks. Why didn't you tell me before I spent all that money on the limo?"

She laughs and leans in to kiss me when a whirr from outside stops her cold. "The garage door. My parents!"

"I thought they were going out for dinner to-night," I say, leaping out of bed, my heart beating like a jackrabbit's.

"That's what they said." Miranda gets up and starts throwing clothes at me. "Get dressed, quick!"

I pull on my underwear and grab my pants. "Throw me my shirt," I call.

She stumbles as she goes to pick up my t-shirt from the floor. I speed-dress, glance in her mirror to make sure there's no traces of lipstick, then notice she's holding her stomach. I frown. "Are you okay?"

"Yeah, just dizzy."

"So," I say, her parents' key turning in the back door lock. "Front door or bedroom window?"

Chapter 7

When I finally go back to mixed martial arts class, Adam is away with the stomach flu, so I manage to make it through the next week and a half with just the regular training bruises. Wednesday, I get home just as Mom walks in behind me with the groceries. While she goes through the mail, I start putting away the cans of spaghetti sauce, beans, and soup.

"Hey," Mom says, "there's a letter for you. It's from the University of Calgary." She tears it open without even handing it to me.

"Um, Mom . . ." I say, peering over her shoulder. "If it's a letter for me, shouldn't I be the one to open it?"

"It's already done," she says casually, taking the paper out and unfolding it. She silently reads it, eyes darting back and forth across the page, breath coming fast, fingers moving to cover her lips. "Oh Cody . . ."

"What?" I snatch the letter from her hand and read it myself. "Hey, my early acceptance went through. Cool."

"How are you going to pay for it?" Mom asks, already reaching for the phone.

"My Bio teacher helped me get a scholarship earlier this year and I can probably find some other funding if I tried. Maybe from the government."

"Doubt it." Mom takes the letter back from me. "It says you need to have an eighty-six percent average. Are you getting that?"

"Close. Don't worry about it," I say in my best Italian gangster accent.

"We have to celebrate! I'm calling your grandma."

Less than an hour later we're at Grandma's place. The kitchen is full of my aunts and Uncle Tom, my sister, and my cousins. The table is laid with various dishes, mostly from the grocery store deli and fast food joints, though my grandma managed to make homemade chili on short notice. I scoop some chili out of a bowl using a bun. It escapes and slops back down, splashing my shirt. Jennie and a few aunts giggle, pointing.

I grab a spoon.

Grandma takes my hand in hers. "Cody, I'm so, so proud of you."

"Thanks," I say, smiling blankly as she says something in our language that I don't understand.

Uncle Tom slaps me on the back. "Mr. Big

Shot, huh? Mr. University. Going to be too good for the rest of us pretty soon."

"Never," I shake my head.

"Naw. You will. You'll get that education and end up somewhere like Toronto."

My stomach drops a little. I haven't told anyone about my University of Toronto application yet. I know they won't want me to go. Before I start feeling too guilty, Jennie comes up and begins to twirl around me, rubbing my head and chanting, "Cody's going to university. Cody wants some tail. Cody's going to university. Cody wants some tail."

I lay on my innocent grin. "You should come to university with me, Jennie."

Jennie jabs her hand on her hip. "Why would I want to go to there?"

"I thought you liked girls too."

She swats me and stalks away.

I resume eating my chili, adding a little hot sauce first.

"I was lucky to finish high school," my mom says, coming up behind me. "It was only because of your grandma and my English teacher that I made it through. You're something else, Cody."

"Did you ever want to go to university?" I ask.

Mom shrugs. "It crossed my mind. My teachers thought I might be one of the ones who would go. But your dad left us just as I graduated. Someone had to work. University . . . it sounds like you'll have fun."

I smile. I can already imagine it. The girls, the

parties, the girls, the sports, the girls, the clubs —
the girls.

My phone makes a little beepy song telling me
I have a text. Mom turns away to give me some
privacy — not that there is much to be had in this
crowded house. I glance at the screen to see who
it is. Miranda. I quickly scroll down, hoping it's
the final details of our plan to hook up tomorrow
night. It says: "Got some bad news. I'm pregnant.
Call me." She ends it with a smiley face.

Sweat rises on my skin and I feel the colour
drain from my face. I'm cold and ill. My pulse
picks up. The chili is no longer happy in my stomach. I slip the phone into my back pocket and
push unsteadily through the crowd, heading for
the bathroom.

Grandma's bathroom is brutally air freshened
with a spray that is supposedly rose scented,
though it smells more like a perfume factory's
chemical waste. I lock the door and lean against it,
staring at the message. At the *text* message. Miranda *texted* me she's pregnant. And put a smiley
at the end. *Who does that?* My breath catches in
my throat as I dial her number. I'm worried that I
won't even be able to talk, but I have to hear this
in person. I have to make sure it's not some sick
joke.

Miranda answers her phone in a hushed voice,
like she's trying to keep whoever is nearby from
hearing her talk. "Cody," she hisses, as a door
clicks behind her.

57

"That text. Are you serious?" I find I'm keeping my voice down too, then I realize it's probably a good idea.

"Yeah, sorry. I was too scared to phone. I . . . I missed my period a couple of days ago and I've been feeling really sick. So I picked up the test from the pharmacy and, well . . ." There's sniffling and a gulp. "I wasn't sleeping around with anyone, I swear. And you and me, we always used condoms. I just don't get it. What could have happened?"

"No idea," I say blankly. I guess condoms really do work only ninety-eight percent of the time. I take a deep breath of thickly-perfumed air and instantly regret it. "So, what now?"

"I've been completely freaking out," she says.

"I hear you," I say, thinking I'm not too far off from that.

Miranda sighs. "I need to look at my options."

"Yeah that's a good idea, we should totally do that. When do you want to get together?"

"Cody, *I* need to look at my options — not you."

"What?"

"I'm —" She gasps. "Oh God."

"It's okay, Miranda. We're in this together," I soothe.

"Not really," she replies, a hard edge coming into her voice. "It's happening to me. My body. Dad is going to kill me, you know."

"Yeah, well I have a whole tribe who are going

to be after me." Her small sniffs pierce my cell. Miranda's crying. I don't want her to cry. Adam might take that as a sign I've hurt her. Then I'm doomed. "It's okay, Miranda, I'm here for you. I'll find a job. I'll look after you. Hell, I'll even marry you, if that's what you want. It will be all right. Don't cry." I'm babbling, trying desperately to say the right thing.

Miranda chokes and coughs. "Yeah, right! Us getting married? I was only joking about that. My dad has no idea I'm not a virgin and you still haven't told your mom about me."

"We could find a way to break it to them." I say it, but in reality I'm sweating and my hands are vibrating at the mere thought of telling my mom I got a girl pregnant, let alone that I'm going to marry her. That would call for a major meeting of the elders. One I don't want to be involved with on any level.

"I have a soccer scholarship," Miranda says. "I've already been accepted to university."

"Me too," I say, picturing my family out there, so proud of me.

"This isn't going to work out," Miranda says.

"Well," I say, "the problem isn't going to disappear. Babies don't just vanish."

"We'll see," Miranda mutters. "Listen, I've gotta go. I've had a rough day and I feel really sick. Just give me some time to figure this out."

"So, when will I hear from you?" I try to keep the whiny, desperate tone out of my voice, but I can tell when I'm being shoved away. Why are girls so difficult?

"I'll call you. Promise."

"Okay. I love you," I say, sounding lame.

She disconnects and I stand there feeling numb, staring at the toilet thinking *That is exactly where my life is heading*.

"Cody, are you okay?" Mom asks, knocking on the door.

"I'm fine. I'll be out in a sec." I shove my cell phone into my back pocket, then splash some water on my face before heading back out.

"You look pale," she says, meeting up with me in the hallway. "Are you sure you're okay? You were in the bathroom for a while."

"I think I might be coming down with something," I lie. I don't want to get into this. Especially not here.

Chapter 8

Thursday, I slink into jiu-jitsu class five minutes late and start stretching. Adam's back. He doesn't look at me or even react to my arrival. It could be that he's working with our instructor, or it could be that he's really mad and just waiting for the right moment to kill me. After all, I haven't only tapped his sister and nearly gotten her arrested — I've gotten her pregnant too. An inward groan escapes. I shouldn't even be here.

The instructor is correcting Adam's technique. To take my mind off things, I pair up with Harbir and start working on takedowns.

Harbir charges, eyes squeezed tight, trying to knock me off balance. The force throws me sideways, and I stumble.

"Pay attention, Manywounds," the instructor calls. "You should have sprawled your way out of that one."

It's true, my thoughts are not entirely on training. Mostly they're on Adam and whether or not he knows about me and Miranda. He still hasn't met my eye. I don't know if that means he knows and he's mad, he suspects and he's mad — or he doesn't know and I'm being paranoid. I wish I could read minds.

We switch partners again. This time I'm paired up with Carlos, practicing chokes. He comes at me from behind, wraps his arm around my neck, and locks his hand onto his other forearm, completing the rear naked choke. I tuck my chin and try to break it, but he's pretty strong and has really good technique. Soon I'm tapping out. After fifteen minutes of practice I'm seeing stars, and we both decide to take a break.

I watch Adam choking Harbir, who has his eyes closed again. Adam's really improved from a year ago. We both started around the same time, but Adam began because he was a huge Georges St-Pierre fan. I only sort of knew who the guy was when I joined up. I know all about him now, of course. Adam told me. He even lent me some DVDs of his fights. Adam and I got paired up a lot when I first started because we were about the same level, though I was way more of a stick-man. We're kind of rivals in the dojo, but I also think we're pretty good friends. I really hope that doesn't change.

Adam comes off for a drink and glares at me. My gut sinks to my knees. He knows, for sure.

"Hi Adam." I smile, my voice going squeaky.

"Hi yourself. What's the big idea, nearly getting my sister arrested?"

"You heard about that, huh?" I'm waiting for the other shoe to drop, for him to punch me in the head for getting his twin sister pregnant. But he doesn't. Adam just stands there, tapping his foot. All he knows about is the cops. Perfect. I decide to see if I can squirm my way out of trouble. "That's old news. Besides, the police let us go with just a warning. No harm done. Right?"

Adam cracks his knuckles in his fist. "It's a good thing our caveman parents aren't on Facebook yet."

"I'm, um . . . sorry?"

"You know, Manywounds, I don't mind if you date my sister. Or even if you and her . . . you know. But if you hurt her, *ever*, you're dead. Got it?"

"Got it." I nod.

"Good," he says, punching my arm, and not in a friendly way.

I'm still rubbing away the bruise when the instructor calls us over for a few matches. I don't get paired up with Adam for a change, which is good, because he still looks like he wants to take my head off. Instead I end up fighting this crazy British guy who joined two months ago. He's super aggressive and loud, but has no technique worth talking about. Right off the bat, I get rocked pretty hard by an accidental elbow. I should have seen it coming, except I chose that moment to glance at Adam. My ears ring. I bite down on the mouthguard and try to keep my footing. Anger builds inside me. I hate getting rocked. Especially when Adam looks like he's enjoying it. The Brit strikes out again, trying to grab me. I hug his arm with both of mine, and swing my legs up into a flying arm bar. We crash to the ground and I lock my left leg under his chin while arching my back and pulling the guy's arm tight to my chest. He taps out, his face red.

"You can only do that because you're so skinny," the Brit complains, before shaking my hand and going to get some water.

Adam's beaming. He gives me a high-five. "Wow, you beat him in, like, fifteen seconds! Great move," he cheers. "I can't believe you survived that elbow!" And just like that, we're friends again.

I scream and yell as Adam takes on Carlos. Carlos is really skilled and soon Adam is the one tapping out.

"Better luck next time, bud," I say, handing him his water bottle. "Good match."

At the end of our workout, we're all drained and shaky. The Brit claps me on the shoulder and apologizes for hitting me. After all, in practice we're not supposed to KO anyone. Throwing a quick glance at Adam, who's deep in a conversation with Carlos, I decide to get out of there fast.

I don't need him changing his mind on letting me off the hook. Besides, once he finds out about Miranda being pregnant, my life is going to be over.

Chapter 9

Schoolwork and test prep seem like the last thing I should be doing, and not just because it's Friday. Every time a teacher talks to me or hands me a pop quiz, it feels like sandpaper ripping down my skin. My insides are a bag of fighting kittens, all scratching and tumbling around.

Miranda hasn't called back yet. She did text yesterday, asking for more time and a bit of space after I called her. I'm not harassing her on purpose. I just want answers. It's been two days.

I'm really trying to figure out how the hell this happened. I mean, we used condoms every single time and Miranda says she hasn't been screwing around — but can I trust her? Maybe she has. She's hot. It's not like guys don't notice that. And she goes to a different school. How am I supposed to know what she does when she's not with me? But still, it's Miranda. The girl who was pretending we were married with kids.

So maybe that's it. Maybe she set me up. Got pregnant on purpose to trap me and keep me from going to a different university. But that doesn't make sense either. She sounded really freaked out about the whole thing. I just don't get it. How could it have happened? *When* could it have happened?

I know the basic math of reproduction. It's on a poster not fifteen feet away from me. The menstrual cycle is usually twenty-eight days and Miranda waited a couple of days after she missed her period to get the pregnancy test . . . I scratch the numbers onto my notebook and then check the calendar on my cell phone. That would put it on . . . the day we got interrupted by the cops. The day I took a torn condom off my wiener and threw it in the garbage.

It didn't tear in my pants. It tore inside Miranda.

Oh man.

The Biology teacher turns off the lights and starts a PowerPoint presentation on human development to help us review for our upcoming test. I put my head in my hands and groan.

Between classes, I text Miranda, delete it, text her again, delete that, then finally send her a lame message that says, "Hi, how are you doing?" Argh! I suck. The screen stays blank. There's no returning message. Nothing. I'm finally forced to put away the phone when Math class starts and I have to wrap my brain around trigonometry.

By the end of my last class, Miranda still hasn't answered my text and I'm having trouble controlling the wild beast that's taken the kittens' place. I text Miranda again, telling her I need to see her or talk to her. No response. Surprise, surprise. I just stare at the stupid little empty screen on my phone and feel my insides burning up. With a metallic crash, I slam my fist into my locker. My knuckles throb, my head pounds, my other hand clenches my cell. I almost throw it, but then rethink that move. I mean, why should I punish myself? I'm not the one being a jerk. But why won't she answer?

I try calling, but it goes straight to voice mail. I leave a message. "Miranda, it's Cody. I just wanted to see how you are. Give me a call." I get my backpack and coat out of my locker and close the door, muttering to myself, "I should just go and see her. Find out what's going on."

I run out and catch the number one bus on Seventeenth Avenue, heading downtown to make the transfer to the number thirteen. The bus pulls to a stop right across from the Bay. Getting off, I nearly run over Silas.

"Hey!" Silas says, looking surprised. He grabs me and pulls me out of the stream of people on the sidewalk. A C-train rumbles by and buses hiss out their heavy fumes. People crowd past us, trying to get from one stop to another, as pigeons flutter down from the rooftops looking for crumbs and lost bits of paper.

"What are you doing here?" he asks.

"I'm about to catch another bus. What are you doing? Skipping school?"

"No . . ." Silas says, turning his gaze to his fingers. "I was getting dishpan hands and trying not to maim myself." He looks up, smiling. "Where are you headed?"

I let out a sigh. "I'm going to see Miranda, my girlfriend." We start walking toward the number thirteen bus stop as I tell Silas all about the mess I'm in.

"You got the text while you were at your grandma's?" Silas whistles. "With the whole family there? Holy crap!"

"Yeah, I know." It feels good to have someone to talk to about all this.

Silas abruptly stops walking. A man behind him has to change course suddenly, making him spill coffee down his shirt. He curses and throws out a few insults before carrying on.

"I don't think you should go," Silas says.

"What?" I ask. "Weren't you listening? She won't return my texts or calls. I need to find out what's going on. I mean, at this point I don't know if I'm going to university next year or giving it up to support a wife and kid. I don't know if her parents know and if *they're* going to look after the kid." I stop. A thought occurs to me. "I don't even know if she's planning on putting the baby up for adoption."

"That's exactly why you shouldn't go to her

house." Silas grabs my shoulders and steers me toward the C-train platform. "First, you don't know if she's home. Second, you don't know if her parents know. And third — how many people are going to want to kill you?"

"But —"

"Right now, I think you should just forget about it," Silas says.

"Forget about it?" I raise an eyebrow.

"Yeah." He nods. "Until she calls you or, at the very least, until you're sure the coast is clear."

I think of Adam's promise to destroy me if I ever hurt his sister. Pregnancy definitely falls into that category. "Okay. So what do I do? Stare at the phone until Miranda calls or my eyes fall out, whichever comes first?"

"Well, as much fun as that sounds," Silas winks, "I was actually thinking of hitting the mall or something. You know, look at girls, mess around."

"I don't know," I say, but I let Silas steer me onto the C-train platform anyway and we take the train to Chinook Station. The mall is three blocks away. We cut between buildings and through the Staples parking lot, heading past Ricky's All Day Grill. Silas spots a bright yellow Ford Mustang. He utters a soft *ooh*, heading over to run his fingers across the hood.

"Now this is a chick magnet," he says.

"Nice car," I agree.

"Not just nice," Silas says in a hushed voice that sounds like he's talking to a timid animal.

"It's beautiful." He peers in the window. "Check the interior. Look at those seats. You could get laid on seats like those. We should totally cruise in this."

"You don't have the key."

"I don't have the key?" Silas says, reaching into his pocket. "I bet I do." He takes out a hacksaw blade that's been rigged up with electrical tape on one end and ground into peaks and valleys on the other. "This should do it."

"Silas . . ." I say, backing away from the car.

Silas slips his gadget into the lock and wiggles it around until there's a quiet click. Then he opens the door. "See? It's nothing."

"This is a bad idea."

Silas puts away the "key" and pulls out his jackknife before hopping into the driver's seat and unlocking the passenger's side door. "Get in," he says.

I open the door. Silas is holding the knife up, ready to smash the starter with the butt. My adrenalin is racing. Nervous sweat has built up on my back and acidic bile burns my throat. "I don't want to steal a car, Silas," I tell him, my hand resting on the polished leather seat, so cool and smooth. "And you don't either. Not if you want to start a restaurant."

"Cody, we're not stealing anything. We're just borrowing. A quick drive, pick up a few girls, then back again before the owner even knows we've been gone. We used to do it all the time when we were fifteen. We never got caught then and we won't be caught now."

"Yeah, I know, but —"

My cell phone starts its beepy song and I look to see who's texting. It's Miranda. She's written, "Come over."

I text back, "On my way."

"Who texted you?" Silas asks.

"Miranda."

"So . . ."

"What?"

"She wants to see you, right?"

"Yeah."

"We have a car," Silas winks.

I huff and get in. "You just drive me there and bring the car straight back," I command.

"Are you kidding?" he whines. "No girls?"

"No girls. Just a quick ride. Okay?"

I know I shouldn't be doing this. I should just take the bus or something. Getting Silas to drive me is a very, very bad idea, but I have to see Miranda, right now. By car it will only be a matter of minutes. By bus — at least an hour. The choice is clear.

Silas nods and raises the butt of his knife, smashing the starter before jamming the blade into the ignition. I turn to close my door and grab my seatbelt when a fist comes out of nowhere and slams me in the cheek, bouncing my head off the dashboard. I catch a glimpse of Silas being hauled out of the driver's seat by a monster of a guy before the fist smashes my eye again and I get pulled out onto the concrete too.

"Steal my buddy's car, will you?" the guy yells as I land face-first on the ground, blood dripping from my nose and grit getting between my teeth.

Holding my face and looking up, I make out the guy who's beating me. He's like a mountain. Even his pinkies are muscular. He cracks his knuckles, obviously planning to hurt me in a way I won't walk away from. My head throbs and slippery blood covers my hands. On the other side of the car, Silas is grunting with each blow this guy's buddy is throwing. I don't know if we're going to make it out of this one alive. I almost wish the police would come.

The massive guy pulls back his leg to kick me. On instinct alone, I reach out and grab it, pushing forward at the same time. The guy loses his balance and tumbles back onto the concrete, hitting his head hard.

He swears and rolls around a bit, giving me enough time to dodge around the car and throw a roundhouse kick to the guy beating the crap out of Silas. The guy, who I figure is also the owner of the car, bends over, grabbing his gut. I yank Silas by the arm and try to pull him up and out of there. He's too dazed to move. It's frightening how much blood covers his face and shirt. There's the scraping of shoes on concrete behind me. A crack of knuckles on my backbone knocks all the breath out of me. My spine blooms with fire-like pain.

I wonder briefly if I'm going to be paralyzed. I fall onto Silas, swearing and kicking. My foot hits the owner's leg. He stumbles and falls. I hiss at Silas, pleading, "Come on! Get up!" His eyes are open, pupils rolled back. I shake Silas and kick out again as the man starts to get up, knocking him back down.

Scrambling, I jerk Silas to his feet. The owner has gotten up again too. He takes a swing at me. I duck and punch, hitting him hard on the chin and knocking him on his ass. Then I run, dragging Silas along with me. The other guy is still on the ground, holding his head. But the owner is not so out of it. He gets up and runs after us. I stop and, using Silas for balance, kick higher than I've ever kicked before, hitting the guy right in the nose and sending him flying backward.

That's when I hear the sirens. I drag Silas through the gap between the pet store and Home Depot, then over to the C-train station. There's a train just pulling in. We hop on and go only two stops before jumping off. I'm sure the cops are going to start searching the trains. We run, trying to put as much distance between us and the station as we can. The adrenalin that helped me out so much in the fight is now making me shaky and weak. I find a bus bench and we both collapse.

Silas looks at me, his face pale and puffy. He lets loose one of his grins. "Some party," he slurs.

"Shut up," I say.

"At least Miranda will like your new look."

Silas tries to wink, but with his eyes swelling shut it looks like more of a leer. "Girls love the bad boy."

"Shut up," I repeat. Miranda is *not* going to love this. Not now.

Chapter 10

I don't sleep well that night. First, because my face feels like it's been through a meat grinder and second, because Miranda probably thinks I've stood her up. I mean, I didn't get to her house and I never called or texted to explain. What could I say? I didn't come over because I got beat up stealing a car? Man, I'm so screwed. I just wish I knew what was going on. I wish I had been able to get over there. Does she have a plan? Has she talked to anyone about this? Is she going to adopt the kid off? Maybe I could get one of my family members to adopt it so I can at least get to see it. I mean, if this kid has half my DNA, I've got to take some responsibility for it.

I'm kind of all freaked and tingly inside at the same time. Like when you're little and waiting to open the Christmas presents and you're hoping it's what you asked for but you're pretty sure it's not. It's that feeling — an excited dread — of *me* becoming a dad. It just blows my mind. I mean, I don't know if I can handle being a dad right now. I'm pretty sure it would mess up everything in my life fairly dramatically. Still, a little Cody running around would be kind of cool. I could be everything my dad wasn't. I could take my kid to powwows and teach him how to ride a horse. Not that I'm all that good at it. Maybe we could learn together. I could teach him how to skateboard. Now *that* would be cool. Get him all dressed up like a mini-gangster and show him how to tag.

I start to think about what I would need to do to prove to Miranda, and eventually my family and her parents, that I'm ready to help. Ready to do this. Ready to be responsible for the mistake that's going to eventually be a human being. Show everyone that I can be a real dad.

I have to get a job.

Nobody would take me seriously if I didn't have one. Just saying you're going to be there to support a girl and a kid without any kind of income is like blowing smoke out your ass. Mom told me that she had to live with her parents when she first had Stella because our dad couldn't find a job. But he was on the reserve. There wasn't much for him there. It was before the casino was built. For me, it's different — I live in the city. We have malls and gas stations and things. This should be easy.

While Mom sings some country hit in the

shower, I sneak into Stella and Jennie's room. The floor creaks. Jennie snorts in her sleep and turns over. Stella isn't home. She's at her boyfriend's. Stealthily, I pull open her makeup drawer. I wish my sister were here to help, because there is no way I'm going to ask Jennie. I would never hear the end of it. It's bad enough that she saw me get home all beat-up yesterday.

I never, *ever* thought I would need to use my sister's makeup.

I search through the dusty containers of eye shadow and smooth black tubes of lipstick, glancing over my shoulder every second to make sure Jennie is still out of it. Finally, I pick a glass bottle labelled *concealer* and a small lipstick-covered mirror and sneak it back to my room, closing the door behind me. Once there, I dab it gingerly on my face, wincing every time I hit a bruise, trying to cover up all the marks. The goop seems to disguise most of the greens, blues, and purples, but my eyes are still puffy and one of them is half-closed. At least my lip has gone back to normal size, even if it does hurt to brush my teeth. I didn't bother with mouthwash this morning. I can only take so much torture.

I'm done just as Mom turns off the water. I grab my hoodie and disappear out the door before she's even out of the bathroom. It's still pretty early, so I go over to Jarrod's house for a bit, waiting until ten o'clock, when the mall opens. He's already up and working on an old US army motorcycle from the 1950s, getting ready to restore it to its original colour scheme. I watch him while drinking coffee and eating a doughnut from the box his dad bought for their breakfast. I catch him up on all the stuff that's happened recently, from the text all the way to Silas and me getting into a smackdown and Mom's gossipy calls to the aunts last night, after she saw the state of my face.

"Silas is going to land his ass back in jail," Jarrod says, taping off a star shape on the gas tank.

"Yeah," I agree. "He's always looking for the next scam."

"And you . . ." Jarrod says, stopping to take a gulp of his coffee, "you need to grow up, especially if you're going to have a kid."

"I do what I want," I counter.

"Humph," Jarrod grunts and goes back to taping. "Man up, dude. Stop waiting for your family to point you in the right direction."

"Easy for you to say, your dad never calls your grandparents on you like my mom does."

"He doesn't have a reason to," Jarrod says, cutting the tape carefully with a utility knife. "I don't get beat up stealing cars."

We sit in silence, listening to the traffic and early-morning birds outside the window. "I'm looking for a job today," I announce.

Jarrod looks up. "With that face? Good luck."

***

At Chinook Centre, I study the job listings I printed off at home. The list is long, and half of them aren't for me. The salon is looking for licensed hair stylists. The chiropractic clinic needs a massage therapist. Even though Miranda really likes my massages, I doubt they will give me a job. In the end, I decide to apply at a skateboard clothing store, Wind Mobile, and the movie theatre, and then try out some of the other stores, depending on how things go.

The guy at the skateboard clothing store smirks. "Are you wearing makeup?"

My face gets hot and I shake my head, wishing Stella had been home to help me. I must have done it wrong.

"Well," he says, letting out a big sigh like talking to me is some kind of burden, "I guess you can give me your resumé and we can have someone look at it."

I go cold. I don't have a resumé. I forgot about that part. Mumbling some lame excuse, I slink out and go to the bathroom to wash off the concealer. Drying off, I go back to the bench where I started, thinking I must be the dumbest person alive.

The thing is, I've never looked for a job before and it shows. Sure, I've worked. Every summer since I was twelve. But only for Uncle Tom, pouring concrete driveways. I calm down and steel myself. I have to do this for Miranda so I can at least talk to her on a level playing field. I have to make this work. This time I head for the Wind

Mobile place. The guy at the counter is happy. A little too happy, maybe. He's like a hopped up camp counsellor telling me how awesome it is to work for these guys. He asks for my resumé and I tell him it's a bit out of date and ask for an application instead. After filling that out, the guy looks it over and nods his head. "This is good," he says. "I'll pass it on to my boss and we'll give you a call."

I almost don't go to the movie theatre, I'm so confident I've nailed the job with Wind Mobile. Still, better safe than sorry. I wander through the mall, past the Bay and the cowboy clothing store. The bookstore looks busy; I bet I could get a job there. I put that on my to-do list and take the escalator up to the movie theatre. At the desk, I ask one of the guys about jobs. He calls his manager, a big Middle Eastern guy with close-cropped hair. "What can I do for you?" he asks.

"I'd like a job application," I reply.

"We don't like trouble," he states.

"Huh?" I ask. "I just want to apply for a job. You know, selling tickets, making popcorn, that kind of stuff."

The guy shakes his head, his eyes not giving anything away. "We don't like trouble."

"I'm not trouble." I have to work hard to keep my voice steady. I just want a stinking job. I'm not here to be judged. "I can sweep, mop, you know, do whatever. I know how to work."

He points, two-fingered, at my face and says,

"You're trouble. Go away."

I want to grab him and show him just what kind of trouble I can be, but a security guard is already heading my way and this guy isn't worth the hassle.

"Thanks for the chat," I say, and stalk to the escalator.

Back at the bench, my stomach starts growling. I've only had a doughnut today and it's getting close to noon. Even from below the food court, french fry grease and spicy tacos fill the air. It's too much. I head up. I'm about to order a burger and some fries from A&W when I hear Miranda's voice.

Chapter 11

I dart past the frozen yogurt place and see Miranda sitting with a few of her friends. The sun through the large window gives her face a radiant glow. Or maybe that's because she's pregnant?

"Miranda. Hey, what a surprise." I'm not sure if she's going to yell at me for last night or just be happy to see me. Maybe both.

"Cody? What are you doing here?" she asks, getting up, her face turning red.

"Looking for a job," I reply.

She grabs my hand and gives it a squeeze, silently begging me not to make a scene in front of her friends.

They stare bullets.

"Cody, we should talk," she says.

"Yeah, good plan," I reply.

Miranda bites her lip and excuses herself. We walk slowly down the mall, pretending to look in the shop windows and not meeting each other's eyes. "So?" I finally say. "You told them, huh?"

"Told who what?"

"Your girlfriends. You told them I got you pregnant."

"No . . . Why do you think that?" Miranda says, taking a sudden interest in a men's tie display.

"No reason."

"You didn't come over last night."

"You didn't return my calls." I hate the sulky tone that has somehow crept into my voice. It sounds so lame.

"I was at the doctor's most of yesterday," Miranda explains, still not meeting my eye. "I couldn't have my phone on in the office. I was so stressed I forgot it was off until way later. I was going to stop by and see you after your MMA practice today. Shouldn't you be there now?"

MMA practice. I'd completely forgotten about it. "I skipped it," I lie.

"I thought you were mad at me."

"Mad?" I shake my head. "I'm here looking for a job so I can support you and the baby, or whatever," I end vaguely.

Miranda lets out a harsh laugh. "You're going to support a baby on a mall job? Right."

"Well, probably not," I admit, "but it gives us options. It could be enough to help you until the baby is born. I was thinking maybe I could talk to some of my relatives. You know, see if they wanted to adopt him or something. Just so he wouldn't be raised by strangers and completely lose his culture. Well, my half of it anyway."

"Him?"

"Or her." I shrug.

Miranda bites her lip, chewing it silently. Finally she says. "Cody, I wasn't at the doctor's yesterday. Well, not the regular doctor's anyway."

"What's that mean?

"I went to an abortion clinic. I'm not keeping the baby."

"You're not?"

She shakes her head.

"But, but . . ." My mind reels. My stomach drops. Abortion. I didn't think Miranda could. Or would. "You don't have to do that," I rasp, my voice giving out.

Abortion. No way.

I clear my throat. "There are better options. I could start university a year late and help you out. I could work and pay rent so you could rest and study."

"Cody," Miranda stops walking. "I can't go to university on a sports scholarship and be pregnant."

"Then start after the baby's born."

"I'll lose the scholarship."

I step forward and point my finger in her face. "I was looking for a job so I could help with things like that. I'm responsible for this too."

"Well, now you don't need to get a job," Miranda says, pushing my finger aside. "You won't be responsible for much longer."

"I bet I can earn enough money to make up for your scholarship," I challenge.

"Really?" Miranda puts her hands on her hips. "Who's hiring you? I didn't want to say anything, but your face looks like crap. What the hell happened?"

"I got into a fight." My brain is whirling. I can't believe that Miranda wants to have an abortion.

"Yeah, I can tell that. How?"

"I got jumped stealing a car." I'm so rattled, I forget to make up a story or even hide my part in it.

"You were stealing a car?" Miranda glares at me.

"Not stealing, *exactly*." I put up my hands in defence, realizing my mistake too late. "More like borrowing. So I could get to you."

"Oh," she scowls, "that's much better. So you want me to raise a kid with a car thief?"

"I told you, I wasn't st—" My temper boils over and I can barely get the words out. "I'm trying!" I snap.

"If you're trying," she retorts, eyes flashing, "why don't you let me get our lives back to normal?"

My stomach lurches at the thought of Miranda willingly destroying something so small and defenceless. "Do you even know what they do in an abortion?"

"Yeah," Miranda nods, chewing on her lower

lip once more. "They told me all about it. They take a little vacuum thing and suck everything out." She touches me on the arm. "It's not that big a deal."

"But you aren't even *asking* me what I want." I stare at her, my brain buzzing, overloaded.

"Why would I ask you?" She raises her eyebrows, confused.

"Because we're in this —"

"We're not. It's my body!"

I turn and kick a nearby garbage can, anger overflowing. A couple of people turn to stare at us. Miranda grabs my arm and yanks it.

"Cody, cut it out. It's really not that big a deal," she hisses.

"Says you. When?"

"When what? Stop being so random!"

"When are you getting it done?"

"Next week sometime. I'm waiting for the test results."

"And you think this is all right?"

"I have no choice!" She punches my arm in frustration.

"You do! Let me help. Or at least ask me my opinion."

"Your opinion isn't going to change anything!"

The pressure explodes from my chest like a big dark storm. I'm full of lightning and thunder, rain and pounding hail. I glare at Miranda, grab my crotch, and thrust it toward her. "Just cut off my balls, why don't you? I know you want me to curl up at your feet like a good little puppy and shut the hell up!" I kick the garbage can again. It rattles under my assault. More people slow down and stare, taking a wide path around us.

Miranda's face goes red. "Shut up! You're making a scene." She grabs my arm and pulls me close, anxiety sour on her skin. She hisses in my ear, "It's not you who has to cover up morning sickness with lame excuses. It's not you who has to carry this thing around for nine months. It's not you who has to take time off to give birth."

"What's nine months? That's less than a year. I could talk to my cousin and his wife. They want kids. We could —"

"We? There is no *we*. Get it through your thick skull!" She lets go and looks at the floor. "Besides, I don't know if I *could* give a kid away after having it inside me for so long."

"But you could kill it?"

"Don't say that!"

"Why? It's the truth. Life is sacred. All life. Even the accidental kind!"

"It's not alive!"

Now it's my turn to pull her toward me and growl into her ear. "If it's not alive, why do you need an abortion?"

"Let me go!" Miranda struggles.

I keep my grip solid, not tight. Not hurting her. "Just let me help. Okay?"

Tears start to crowd her eyes. "Let go."

"Fine!" I throw up my hands spinning and

smashing the garbage can with a roundhouse kick, making a rattling boom echo down the mall. "You've decided. That's it, that's all!"

Miranda nods.

"And nothing I say can change your mind?"

"No," she says quietly. "I don't need your permission."

"Fine," I snarl. "At least let me go with you."

"Why?"

"I told you, it's my responsibility too. I should at least witness the death of our child."

"Stop saying things like that!"

"No! It's the truth!"

Miranda shakes her head. "My parents aren't even coming. They don't know about any of this. I just want to get it over with."

"Are you going to at least tell me *when* it's happening?" I feel like I'm begging. It's so stupid. "Am I allowed to know that much?"

"Fine, Cody." Miranda sighs heavily, her colour drained, the glow gone. "I promise I'll tell you when I book the appointment. Okay?"

"Okay."

She gives me a thin smile. "Why can't you be like a normal guy, huh? Just happy to be done with it."

"Not all guys are like that, Miranda. And if you think so, you don't know us at all."

"Trust me, Cody. It's better this way." Miranda goes up on her tiptoes to kiss me on the cheek. I don't respond. I just stand there like a frozen piece of meat. She wipes her eyes with the back of her hand, then heads off to rejoin her friends.

I pace back and forth, my head pounding. People are staring. It irritates me. I kick the garbage can again and again trying to get rid of this horrible lost feeling that's eating me from the inside.

Two security officers come up and grab me by the shoulders, pulling me back. "Sir, we're going to have to ask you to leave."

I glare at them, wanting to punch them both in the head. "I just came to look for a job," I say. "I was just trying to do the right thing!"

"Not today, sir," the blond rent-a-cop says. "It's time for you to go."

As I'm marched out of the mall, I meet the eyes of the Wind Mobile guy. He shakes his head, picks up a piece of paper from his desk, and drops it in the trash behind him.

Chapter 12

All the way back to my neighbourhood, I can't focus on anything. My mind is playing a loop of all the horrible things that have happened to me today. The skateboard store guy and the movie theatre moron, the Wind Mobile guy throwing my application in the garbage, and Miranda — stupid Miranda telling me she's going to have an abortion. Not asking. Not even giving me a chance to prove I'm good enough for her and the baby. God, I hate her. I can't believe I ever became her boyfriend. I must have been blind. Or maybe I really am stupid.

I head back over to Jarrod's place. Silas is hanging out in the living room, watching a movie. "Cody!" he says, grinning. "You look like you came out okay."

Silas looks way worse than I do. He has two black eyes and his face is pretty mottled with swelling and bruising.

"I guess."

Silas frowns. "You look like someone stole your lollipop. Everything okay?"

"Fine," I mutter.

I just can't take Silas right now. I need quiet. I need oblivion. I head to the kitchen.

Jarrod's sitting at the table sketching a lit candle. He doesn't look up. "So, how'd the mall go?"

"Miranda was there. We got in a fight. The rent-a-cops kicked me out. Everything sucks."

Jarrod flicks his head toward the fridge. "Grab a drink. Sit down."

I pull open the old fridge and push aside the pop to get at the beer. It's cold in my hand and water droplets immediately form on its surface. I crack open the top and down the whole thing in one go, grabbing another before the fridge closes.

"That bad?" Jarrod asks.

"She's going to have an abortion."

"That works," he says, not looking up from his drawing. "No problems for either of you."

"But what if I don't want her to have one, eh?" I ask.

"Then you're stupid," Jarrod replies.

The back door opens and Taylor Manyguns and his crew crowd in. "Let the party begin!" Taylor shouts, going into the living room and turning off the TV to the shouts of Silas. A minute later, Winnipeg's Most is blasting from the stereo.

I grab my beer and head to the living room to drink it. Soon, more and more people show up. It

92

turns out Jarrod's dad has left town to deliver a car to Fort McMurray, so Silas organized a party. I sit, drinking beer after beer, and watch everyone rapping and dancing. I'm not really enjoying the party, but I don't feeling like getting up and leaving either. Miranda calls once, but doesn't leave a message. I don't answer, I just turn off my cell. If Miranda can shut out the world, so can I. Besides, she made her views pretty clear. I should shut up and do what I'm told. No opinion. No backtalk.

The bright blue of day blurs into the purple of evening and a new crowd of people arrive. Carly Yellow Horse, smelling of black liquorice and bubble gum, strolls in with her brother Jacob and some of their friends. Carly comes and sits on my lap, wrapping her long arms around my neck and planting a sticky lipstick kiss on my cheek. "Hey Cody, what happened to you?"

"Silas," I joke.

"Looks painful. Maybe you need a nurse," she says, pushing her hand under my shirt and rubbing my chest. "I've missed you."

"Yeah?" I ask, grabbing her around her slim waist and remembering how good she felt in the back of her dad's van.

"Oh yeah," she says, then kisses me, tongue and all.

She's so warm and inviting, and I am so drunk and turned on. A thought occurs to me. "I have a girlfriend now," I say when we come up for air.

"Since when?" Carly snaps, pulling back.

I realize my mistake and quickly clear up her confusion. "Not very long. A couple of months after we hooked up."

"I thought *we* were going to be boyfriend and girlfriend. I mean, I wouldn't have made out with you otherwise." She scowls and looks away. "You never even called me afterward."

"Your father chased me across a snowy field in my ginch! I took it as a sign."

A small smile reappears on Carly's lips. "So, I'm guessing your girlfriend isn't around right now." Her brown eyes scan the room.

I shake my head. "No. We had a fight."

"Well then, let me help you feel better," Carly says, kissing me some more. "My dad's not here."

Blood pushes through my body, fast and firm. She feels so good and I'm tired of feeling bad. I pull Carly closer. She giggles in response, straddling me and pushing her chest against mine. Her breasts move up into my face, where she wiggles them back and forth. "So, what do you think? Want to see why we should be together?"

It doesn't take much persuasion to get me into Jarrod's bedroom, the bedsprings squeaking. Luckily, I found condoms in his bedside table. I don't need to be in two messes. When we finish, Carly starts kissing me all over and takes cell phone pictures of us lying naked in bed. I'm barely paying attention. I'm already feeling guilty about the whole thing. My mind keeps jumping to Miranda. Her body, her smile. Yeah, we had a fight, but neither one of us said it was over. Not really.

"I've got to go," I tell Carly, slipping back into my clothes. "I have some things to work out."

It's nearly one in the morning by the time I stumble home. I'm pretty blitzed and a cold north wind only makes me more miserable. I think I even feel the odd snowflake. Spring in Calgary is a very uncertain thing. Kind of like my life. One minute I'm on top of the world, going to university, getting the girl, going to win at the jiu-jitsu tournament. Next I've got a girl pregnant, my well-thought-out life is falling apart, and I'm powerless to do anything about it.

I try to match my key to the front door lock, but keep missing in the dark. Finally, after a few curses, I succeed in opening the door. I stumble into the house, bump into the side table with my hip — upsetting a vase of roses — and stumble to my room. Maybe things will look better in the morning.

Chapter 13

Sleep doesn't come. I lie in bed, hands behind my head, staring at the ceiling. The entire day keeps playing over and over — the job hunting, the fight with Miranda, and Carly's sweet body in my arms. Guilt about Carly swamps me. Some father I'd be. I can't even be true to my girlfriend. Maybe I'm not cut out to have a kid. Then again, I can't believe Miranda would kill a baby. *Our* baby. My heart starts pounding in a wash of adrenalin. I have to stop her. I can't let her do this. I wish I could think of a plan that would actually work. Something I could say or do that would change her mind.

It would help if my brain wasn't so sloshy.

Then it comes to me. Dad. Okay, maybe he wasn't around much growing up, but he always said to call him if I ever needed anything. This definitely falls into the category of anything. I get up and grab my cell phone, dialling his number.

It rings six times before he answers. "What's up, Cody?" It sounds like he's at a bar or a party, with all the whooping and loud music in the background.

"Dad, I got a girl pregnant." I'm too drunk to find a gentle way of telling him.

"Oh, jeez. Does your mom know?" he asks.

"Are you kidding?"

"Right. No. Okay, so you knocked up a girl and now . . . "

"She's getting an abortion," I say.

"Well, that's good news."

"No, Dad."

"No? Cody, you don't want a kid."

"I know, but I don't want it killed either."

"What do her parents say?"

"She hasn't told them."

"So she's keeping this under the table too, eh?" Dad says. "Cody, just take this as a blessing. Seriously, if your mother had an abortion the second time she got pregnant, I might have stuck around. She was going to, but then her parents found out and *bam*, the next thing you know she's buying baby clothes and picking out names." Dad burps long and loud. "Frickin' parents."

"Dad," I say.

"Yeah?"

"That second baby — that was me."

There's a pause, then, "Oh right, sorry about that. Love you, son."

"Sure, Dad. Bye."

"Bye Cody. Don't be a stranger," he says, hanging up.

I lie there, thinking. Interfering parents, eh? I might have just found a way to stop Miranda from getting an abortion. I get my shoes on. Drunk or not, it's time for a late-night trip.

***

Buses don't run at two in the morning, and I live too far away to walk to Miranda's, so I grab a jacket, steal forty bucks out of my mom's purse, and sneak outside to call a cab. I'm not waiting until I sober up to get the job done. I need to do this now, while I still have the nerve and things are clear in my head.

The cab arrives five minutes later. In another twenty minutes, I'm at Miranda's house. I pay the cabbie and get out. As he pulls away, I realize I don't have enough money to get home. It doesn't matter. This is a mission to save a life.

The windows of the house are dark and the wooden front door looks thick. The snow has turned to icy drizzle and the wind is kind of sobering me up. A dog barks in the distance and two cats yowl in a fight. I feel like a warrior, ready to go into battle. I stride up to the porch and ring the doorbell, then pound on the door for good measure.

"Mr. Blake!" I finally yell. "Mr. Blake, do you

know what your daughter is doing?"

It takes a while, but Miranda's dad, a short, balding man with a cookie-duster moustache and pot-belly, opens the door. His face is red and his jowls jiggle with barely-contained rage. He holds a golf club like a sword, ready to defend his family.

"Cody?" His expression changes to bewilderment as he recognizes me. "What are you doing here?" He wrinkles his nose. "Are you drunk?"

"Yes!" I confirm. "But it's Miranda's fault."

"What?" he asks, looking more confused. "Miranda's been home all night."

I stick my finger in the air, making my point while things are still going so well. "I got your daughter pregnant and now she's having an abortion!"

The confusion leaves and Mr. Blake returns to purple rage. "You did *what*?"

"I got your daughter pregnant and now —"

"Miranda?" he asks, striding forward in his slippers, club raised. "You got *my* Miranda pregnant? But she's still a virgin."

"Not so much." I clarify, trying to steer him to the key point, arms crossed defensively above my head. "She wants to have an —"

I don't get to finish because the golf club comes whistling by my ear. I duck unsteadily and crash into the lilac bushes that edge one side of the walkway.

"Dad, stop!" Miranda flies to her father, grabbing his arm. She clings to it, her eyes huge. She looks from him to me and back again. "What's going on?"

"This little punk got you *pregnant*?" Mr. Blake thunders.

Miranda lets go of her dad and strides over to me. With a rock-hard thump, she pushes me back into the bush just as I get to my feet. "Thanks a lot, Cody," she growls.

"I was only thinking," I explain, fighting once more to get out of the bush, "your parents should know. They're your *parents*, after all." I try to throw on my clean-as-the-driven-snow smile, but I'm pretty sure it comes out as a drunken leer.

"So you told your mom too?" Miranda snarls.

"Of course," I lie.

"Is it true?" Mr. Blake asks, turning to Miranda.

"Cody got you pregnant?" Adam asks, appearing with Mrs. Blake, Miranda's mom, on the porch. Adam is bare-chested and in his shorts, iPhone in hand. Mrs. Blake has her arms crossed tight around her dressing gown, blond hair sticking out like antennae, a scowl drawn on her face.

"Well?" Mrs. Blake demands.

Miranda turns from one face to another and starts crying. "I was going to tell you all," she pleads, tears glistening. "I was. I just . . ." she looks at me, eyes blazing, voice growling, "needed more time."

"Yeah, time to get an abortion." I look to Mr. and Mrs. Blake for support. They'll stop her. I know it.

"You were going to get an abortion?" Mrs. Blake asks, opening her arms to her daughter. "Without telling us? Oh, honey. How terrifying."

"I was so scared!" Miranda cries, running to her mother.

Mr. Blake throws down the club and charges at me, fist raised. "You little bastard!"

I duck and roll, falling untidily on the wet ground.

Mrs. Blake glares, clutching Miranda tight to her chest. "How dare you make her get an abortion by herself?"

"I was trying to st—"

Mr. Blake advances again. "You were trying to get her pregnant!" he thunders. "What?"

"No, you jerk!" I yell, anger making my words rattle. "The condom broke."

"What? When?" Miranda asks, letting go of her mother and moving toward me.

"The night the cops nearly arrested us."

"You got my daughter arrested?" Mr. Blake raises his fist once again and leaps forward. "I'll kill you!"

"No, Dad!" Miranda shrieks.

Adam jumps on him, pulling him back.

"*Nearly* arrested!" I yell. My adrenalin isn't mixing too well with the beer in my bloodstream. My stomach rolls and gurgles. "We were making out in the SUV and the cops interrupted us," I try to explain.

Mrs. Blake frowns. "It sounds like you were

doing a little more than making out."

"You little prick!" Mr. Blake cries out, fists clenched. He breaks free of Adam and charges, his knuckles slamming into my ear.

The ground rushes up at my head. A dizzy sickness twists through me. Icy, wet grass soaks my clothes.

Mrs. Blake gasps.

"Dad, don't!" Adam jumps on him again, grabbing at his arms. "Let me deal with it."

"I just wanted to let you know," I plead, staggering once more to my feet. "I just wanted you to stop her."

"Stop her?" Mrs. Blake asks.

"From having the abortion," I explain.

"Cody, she has a sports scholarship. She can't have a baby right now."

"I told you!" Miranda spits.

Directing her husband toward the house, Mrs. Blake calls to Miranda. "Come on, dear. Let Adam take care of this."

Mr. Blake is breathing hard. He snatches up his golf club and waves it over his head, his wife still blocking him. "If you ever, *ever*, come back to this house, I won't let anyone stop me from hurting you!"

"Dad, please! Go inside and look after Miranda," Adam soothes.

Mr. Blake growls, "Defend your sister, son."

With everyone inside, Adam closes the front door and leans against it, cracking his knuckles and glaring. "Cody, you're a real jerk. You know that, right?"

"I just wanted . . ." I start to walk toward him but end up losing my balance and falling over, still dizzy from Mr. Blake's blow.

"If you weren't so drunk I'd kick the crap out of you."

I scowl at him from the ground. "Why should that stop you? Come on!" I push myself to my feet and put up my fists, stumbling to the side a bit.

"You need to sober up. I already called your mom. She's on her way."

"Thanks a lot," I sneer.

"And Cody," Adam says, opening the door to his house and stepping in. "You and I are done as friends." He closes the door. The lock clicks.

I give them all the finger and start walking home, freezing and wet. I don't care. I sure as hell am not going to wait around for my mom to come and get me.

I've been walking for about half an hour when Mom pulls up beside me in her car. She rolls down the window and calls my name.

"Leave me alone," I say.

"Cody, what is going on with you?"

"Nothing." I stop. My ear aches, my clothes are frozen, and I just want to lie down and forget this whole day happened. Forget what a failure I am.

"Come on," she says, leaning across and pushing open the passenger door.

I give in. It takes a few tries to pull my seat belt

across and get it clicked shut.

"Cody," she says again.

I look out the window, head in my hand, staring at the passing streetlights as Mom pulls away.

"Where were you all day?"

She looks at me. I see her reflection in the side window. I don't turn around.

"I was worried," she says. "Especially when your friend from jiu-jitsu said you were drunk and yelling outside his house."

She stops, waiting for me to speak. I stay silent.

"Come on, Cody. What's wrong? You can talk to me."

I shake my head.

"Were you trying to break into their house?"

I glare at her and turn away again.

"I don't want to have to guess," she says. "Does this have something to do with that fight you got into? Was Silas up to his old tricks?"

"I can get in just as much trouble without Silas," I say, still not looking at her.

"Clearly," Mom replies. "Are you sure you don't want to tell me what's going on?"

"No," I say. "I can handle this on my own."

Chapter 14

I spend all of Sunday in my room on the computer. Mom tries to talk to me a few times. So do a steady stream of relatives who drop by throughout the day, supposedly for tea. I just ignore them and surf the web.

Getting hungry, and not wanting to face the aunts, I dig around in my backpack for a power bar. My hand closes on the crumpled pamphlet I shoved in there after Silas and I ran into that demonstration by my school. The pamphlet isn't pro-choice like I thought. It's for the pro-life side, the one the old guy must have been repping.

I type in the website from the pamphlet and look at the menu. There's a bunch of reading and some videos. I opt for the videos. The mini-movies are professional, with good-looking people talking about when life begins and the truth about abortion. The first one I see has an eight-week-old fetus being arranged with tweezers on a quarter to show how small it is. The next video has a guy talking about his girlfriend getting an abortion and how he found it so upsetting that he started doing drugs and throwing up six times a day. The last video I watch is of an actual abortion with a little severed arm appearing. It freaks me out. It's like a slasher movie — scary, but you can't look away. Miranda might not like the word "kill." But according to these people, that's exactly what she's doing.

I decide to see if I have any rights as a dad. I mean, if she were to have this kid, I would have to pay child support. I couldn't just walk away. Hell, I could even get custody. The courts could make Miranda give me the kid half the time or something. So, if I have those rights when the kid is born, I must have rights while it's still being made.

An hour later I find the answer is no. Men do not have any rights until the baby is born. So even though it's half mine, with my DNA creating it, Miranda can have it pulled out of her and thrown in the trash without even asking me. I pound on the keyboard and wrap my arms around myself. This is so frustrating. This is so unfair!

Then I come up with a new tactic. One Silas accidently taught me. I sign Miranda up for every pro-life newsletter I can find. There are a lot of them. Quite a few are the bible-thumping kind, but I don't care. I want her to admit that what she's doing is wrong. I want her to see the truth about abortion. I want her to stop and think.

After an hour of giving out her e-mail, I stumble onto a medical site. They have a bunch of detailed information about these abortions. They sound horrific. A tube is inserted inside the womb and a syringe sucks the fetus out. The site goes on to say that abortion can cause bleeding, infection, and damage to the organs. I read one paragraph that describes bleeding so bad it makes the woman die. I click on a link and read about the emptiness that some girls experience. How they regret what they've done and get depressed. Some even try to commit suicide. Miranda must be really messed up to want to do that to herself. Or else really scared to have this kid. It makes me worry about how she's going to cope with this.

I keep clicking, finally coming across teen pregnancy stories of girls who kept their kids. The more I read, the more confused I get. The girls talk about how afraid they were. How their boyfriends dumped them and took off. A bunch of the stories end with the girls living with their moms, dropping out of school, or living on welfare. I don't want that for Miranda either.

I end up leaving the computer and lying down on my bed. My head is still pounding from last night's booze. I think about calling Miranda. But what would I say? Sorry I want you to give up your future so that you don't murder a kid we accidently made together? I wish I could just make this whole thing go away. I guess that's what she wants too.

Rolling over, I reach out and grab an info folder for the University of Toronto off my floor. I can't wait to escape. I really hope my acceptance comes soon. I just want to get away from all this — and moving halfway across the country should do it. I flip to the Biology department section. Start reading about the programs. A happy thrill rushes through me at the thought of doing something other than worrying about pregnant girlfriends.

"Pretending you're Mr. Big Shot again?" Jennie says, opening the door to my room.

"Forget how to knock?" I growl.

She sits on my bed. "University is stupid."

"Go away." I give her a shove.

She pushes back, her long nails scraping my arm, and snatches the folder out of my hand. "My brother used to look at these things too, before he went. He thought he was going to be something."

"I *am* going to be something." I snatch it back. "A lot more than you."

"Don't count on it."

"What do you know?"

"You *know* what I know." Jennie frowns, pulling her knees up to her chest. "If my brother had stayed home he might still be around."

"University didn't kill your brother."

"No. The jerks who thought it would be funny to get an Indian drunk did. He was just like you. Into girls. Into partying. Trying to fit in." She looks at me, her cheek on her knee. Her brown eyes going a little pink around the edges.

"I hardly drink. Why would anything change?"

"Because you'll be away from us. Away from anyone who might call you on it."

"I'm not like that."

"Neither was he."

"I can handle it."

"I hope so, Cody, because if the rumours I've heard lately are true, your judgment hasn't been the greatest." She gets up and walks over to my computer. With the click of the mouse, she opens up the Internet browser and scrolls through my history. A list of pro-life and teen pregnancy sites burn on the screen. "So it *is* true. Ha!"

"You little —" I roar, jumping up and grabbing her arm.

She pulls my fingers off her skin and flips her hair over her shoulder. "You make it too easy." She gives me a smug grin.

"You didn't come to warn me about university," I say. "You just came to spy!"

"A little of both," Jennie admits with a wink, turning away.

I lunge for her but she's already slipped out the door, and I know I'll only be playing her game if I follow.

Chapter 15

My messed up weekend finally ends and Monday begins in a haze. Half the time, I don't even realize I'm at school. I can't focus with thoughts of Miranda killing our baby running around in my skull. The only thing that gets my brain in gear is when I pick up the mail after school. The letter I've been waiting for, with the University of Toronto's coat of arms on the envelope, has finally arrived. Luckily, Mom is still at work and Jennie isn't home.

With shaking fingers, I open it and scan the words. My mouth is dry. I'm trembling, but it's good news — my application went through. I have options now. I can get away from my gossiping aunts and annoying cousin. I can try to do things on my own. Be my own person. And I know — I *absolutely* know — that I'm not going to do anything stupid when I get there. I can handle the parties and the clubs. I can handle the girls and the classes. Even if I can't, the more I think about Miranda's decision to end the life of our child, the more I want to leave and never come back, no matter what the price.

After school on Tuesday, I head up to the dojo for my jiu-jitsu lesson. I'm so fixated on my problems with Miranda that I even forget Adam is going to be there. It's not until I see their dad's SUV pulling to a stop right beside me that my brain snaps into focus.

Miranda glares from the driver's seat and jumps out onto the concrete, the vehicle still running. "Cody!" she screams, punching my chest. "WHAT . . . THE . . . HELL?"

I look at her blankly.

"Why didn't you tell me the condom broke?" Miranda's voice is clipped and angry.

"I thought it happened after we had sex," I explain. "From wearing it in my pants for so long."

"You idiot! You should have told me anyway."

"What difference would it have made?"

"I could have taken a morning-after pill. Then none of this would have happened." She crosses her arms, furious.

"What's a morning-after pill?" I ask, dazed.

"It keeps you from getting pregnant, dummy!" Miranda shouts.

"Really?" I say. "I didn't even know they had something like that."

"Even more reason to tell her," Adam calls,

getting out of the vehicle and coming over.

"I asked you," Miranda says, thumping my chest again. "I asked you and you told me you had no idea. You are such a liar! A liar and a cheater. Who is she? Huh? Who were you screwing?"

My head spins with the sudden change of topic. "What?"

Miranda takes a deep breath and slows down like she's talking to a really little kid. "I was on Facebook and I saw pictures . . . tagged . . . of you . . . naked . . . with some girl."

"Carly," I groan.

"Oh," Miranda says, faking perkiness, "is that her name? It's nice to know who you're cheating on me with."

"It was a mistake!" I say, stepping forward.

"Oh yeah?" Adam says. "The same mistake as giving my sister's e-mail to every pro-life spammer out there? What happened that time? Your finger slip?"

I plead. "I just wanted Miranda to see —"

"My inbox jammed with bible-thumper garbage and pictures of dead babies?" Miranda hits me in the chest again. "Thanks a lot."

"I wanted you to change your mind!" I say, stepping back.

"Not the way to do it!" Miranda goes to punch me once more. I catch her fist, but quickly drop it as Adam takes a step forward.

"Life has value," I say.

"Crap, you sound just like them."

"That doesn't make me wrong."

"My life has value too, you know, Cody." Miranda paces. "I don't want to get stretch marks or sagging boobs."

"Do you know how selfish you sound?" I ask.

"Me, selfish? Okay, let's say I have this baby. You still get to go to university. And me, even if I adopt it off, I lose my scholarship and I'll be a year behind. Cody, you are the dumbest guy I've ever dated."

"Okay! I'm stupid! I really thought that when you saw how bad abortion was you'd change your mind and give me a chance."

"A chance to do what?" she asks. "To cheat on me with even more girls? I still can't believe you did that the same day we talked at the mall!"

"We weren't *talking* at the mall. Remember? You were telling me I didn't have a say."

"Well, you don't," Miranda says, hands on her hips. "It's my body —"

"Our baby."

"No! It's not a baby! I've looked it up. It's an embryo. That's it! It has no arms, no legs, and *it's not a baby*! It's just a group of cells that I'm going to get rid of!"

I stand there, stunned.

"How many times, Cody?" she says softly.

"What?" I'm lost again.

"How many times have you cheated on me?" She starts pacing. "Are there more photos? Was she the only one?"

"Yes," I'm stammering. "It was only that time. I was upset. You were being so unfair and I wanted —"

"Sex?" she asks.

"Comfort," I explain, my voice going squeaky. "But it was wrong," I say quickly. "Really, really wrong."

"Well, finally something you understand." She looks over to Adam, then back to me before jabbing her finger into my chest. "If I ever had second thoughts about having this abortion, they're all wiped away now. You wanted a chance to prove yourself, Cody? Well, good job. Now everyone knows you're a lying, cheating, big-mouthed jerk."

Miranda pokes me once more and then climbs back into the SUV. As she drives away, she yells out the window to Adam, "Kick his jiu-jitsu ass for me, bro!"

I glare at Adam and he glares right back at me.

"That was a dirty trick, telling our parents she was pregnant," Adam says. "She would have told them on her own."

"I doubt it. I was trying to make her do the right thing."

"You can't force people to do what you want, you know. It doesn't work that way."

"Oh yeah?" I ask. "It seems to work for everyone else."

"Leave my sister alone or I'll finish what we started Saturday night," Adam threatens.

"Why wait? I'm sober now," I reply, crooking my finger at him. "Chicken?"

"I have jiu-jitsu," Adam turns and heads inside and up the stairs.

I kick a pebble across the parking lot. I don't get it. I was trying to do the right thing. Fix the mess I made in the best way I knew how. I was willing to sacrifice. Willing to admit I was wrong. So how the *hell* did I end up the villain?

After pacing the parking lot, trying to get rid of the agitation rocketing around inside me, I head up to the dojo. There are a few guys already inside, playing soccer on the mats. Adam is hanging toward the back, next to Carlos. I decide to ignore him and pretend that this is a normal class.

I've just finished getting changed when the instructor calls us to circle up and stretch out. My muscles are really tight. Using them gives me a rush that makes me smile for the first time in days.

"Holy crap, Manywounds," the instructor whistles. "What happened to your face? I hope it wasn't you that started it." Right on the first day of class it was pounded into us that jiu-jitsu was just for the dojo, unless you were in danger. Then it was only for escape, nothing more. "It's a noble art," the instructor told us. "Treat it as such."

"I got jumped at the mall. It was purely defensive. Promise."

"Be careful where you hang out," the instructor says, before telling us all to do eight lengths of bear crawls.

After warming up, we review some basic grappling skills, starting with sprawling and back spins. I'm with Carlos for these. He's fast — too fast. I end up on my butt when I'm supposed to be throwing my feet back and my chest onto his shoulders, spinning for the rear naked choke. Adam's struggling too, falling and slapping the mat. Finally the instructor calls a stop to the drill and we all get some water.

Once we're back, the instructor says, "Just a reminder, there's a tournament this month and I want our team to do well. So let's practice. Adam, Cody, let's see if one of you can grapple your way to a submission."

Adam starts to say something, then shuts his mouth. I go to my bag and get my mouth guard. Adam does the same, meeting me on the mats. The timing buzzer goes off and the instructor yells, "Three minutes. Do it!"

Chapter 16

I dive for Adam's legs and he tries to wrap his arm around my neck, sprawling his feet back and out of my way. Adam's grip isn't that good, so I twist and roll around his body, ending up behind him. Our bare feet squeak on the mats and already our breath is coming in puffs. I can smell the musk of his sweat; it slides from his hair across my cheek. I grab his neck and try to lock in. Adam grips my arm, pushing his elbow into my gut, hard. He ducks behind me, holding my shoulder at a really bad angle. I won't tap out. Not to him. Not today. I sweep my leg back, making him lose his position. We face each other, glaring. We both know this is it, this is the fight we were meant to have Saturday night.

Adam comes at me and we lock heads. I spin on his back, but he escapes. We clash again, and this time he goes for the takedown. I try to sprawl and grab his neck, but he's faster and latches onto my ankle, pushing me down and going for the mount. I use my leg and thrust him off. Maybe a bit too hard. Adam grunts.

"Easy, boys," the instructor warns.

He jumps back on me, elbow first. This time, I'm the one grunting. I manage to push him off sideways and kneel up by his head, going for the arm bar. Swinging my leg over, onto his neck, I slam it down hard.

"Slow it down," the instructor says.

Adam rolls free and away. We stand up and circle each other. Adam kicks his foot out and into my gut, knocking me into the wall. Then it's on. I push Adam to the ground, punching and pounding. He gives back as much as I'm handing out. The fight seems to take forever. It seems like we both lay a hundred punches on one another, knuckles cracking and forearms bruising. Really, it's probably only a few seconds before our instructor and Carlos have us both in unbreakable holds and separated to opposite sides of the mat. I struggle, trying to get back to the fight. Adam, not holding still either, spits out his mouth guard and yells, "I told you, Manywounds, if you hurt her I would kill you."

"Yeah, you and your sister are really into killing things aren't you?" I shout back.

"Leave my sister alone!"

"Not until she listens to me!"

The instructor kicks me out first, keeping Adam

back until he's sure I've left the area. My nose is throbbing and my knuckles are cut. There's some swelling above my eye. Adam managed to rock me pretty hard, the jerk.

Both Adam and I were told the same thing. Until we can come to class, apologize, and leave our problems at the door, both of us are out. I'm so mad, it doesn't even faze me.

I decide to walk to Jarrod's. A cool wind is gusting and dirty-looking clouds threaten rain. I zip my hoodie closed and put my head down, trying to keep the stinging dust out of my eyes.

"Hey, it's the Chief!" someone yells behind me. "Chief! Hey Chief!"

I look up and see the Viking with a few of his friends. I stop and wait for them to walk over to me.

"Buddy!" the Viking says, wrapping his arm around my shoulder and laughing. "How have you been? Man, has someone been using your face for target practice?"

"What do you want?" I glare, still itching to fight.

"I thought we could party with you," the Viking says. "You look like someone who knows how to have some fun."

"Yeah," his buddies all join in.

"Besides," the Viking goes on, brave with his gang around, "I owe you for almost breaking my arm."

"If I wanted to break your arm," I say, "you'd be wearing a cast."

The Viking's buddies *ooh* at this statement.

"Come on, Chief. Show us what you Indians can do. Dance or something. Sing." The Viking puts his hand to his mouth and starts to make *woo woo* sounds. "Entertain us. Maybe you can show us some of your slick martial arts moves, huh? Five against one. You're tough enough for that, right?"

"Whatever you want." I'm pumped with the invitation. I already picture myself grabbing the Viking by the head, pulling him down, and slamming his stupid face into my knee when I feel four hands grab onto my shoulders.

"Sorry," Silas says, appearing beside me and holding me back. "Chief Woo Woo can't play today."

"No," Jarrod nods, clutching my other side. "He has an appointment with our medicine man, Doctor Woo Woo."

The Viking and his buddies step forward, looking like they want to take us all on.

Silas looks at them, eyebrow raised. "I could let him go, you know. You do realize Cody's a fifth-degree black belt. Won a death match at the International Mixed Martial Arts Cage Tournament in Thailand last year. Killed a man. He'll probably wipe the sidewalk with you." Silas peers into my face. "Yeah," he nods, "that's the only kind of playtime you're going to get out of your Chief today. Interested?"

The Viking looks nervous. He steps back. "You're lying."

Silas makes a show of letting me go. "Let's find out."

I pump my fist and throw out a cat-in-heat yowl. They back up further.

Silas stomps at the little gang. "Scram," is all he says.

The Viking and his buddies jog away, grumbling, while Jarrod, hands still on my shoulder, steers me in the opposite direction.

"I'm a yellow belt," I say to Silas a block later. "And I've never competed in any kind of death match."

"What did you want me to say?" Silas shrugs, getting into a Bruce Lee fighting stance. "Fear my yellow belt! I won second place in a local competition against a bunch of fifteen-year-olds!"

I laugh. "Okay, you have a point."

"It's a good thing we spotted you when we did." Jarrod grins. "I think we may have just saved some lives. What's got you so pissed off?"

I give them the rundown of Saturday night and the fight at the dojo. By the time I'm done with the story, my insides have calmed down and I'm almost sorry for beating on Adam. Almost.

We get back to Jarrod's house and settle into the shelter of the backyard. Jarrod grabs some Cokes and tosses one to me. "Why the hell do you want a kid so bad?" he asks. "Are you nuts?"

"I don't. I just want . . . I don't know . . . someone to listen. Why don't I get a say?"

"Because you're not the one who's pregnant,

121

stupid," Jarrod says.

"But it's mine."

"Not until it's born," Jarrod kicks at my chair. "You're acting like a lunatic."

"I don't care," I sulk.

Silas grins. "Yeah, that's kind of obvious." He reaches into his pocket and pulls out a packet of beef jerky. "Want some? Freshly lifted."

Jarrod shakes his head. "You guys are such idiots."

"Says you," Silas retorts.

"Yeah, says me," Jarrod returns. "You keep stealing and Cody can't get his priorities straight."

"Screw you," I say.

"Does your mom know about Miranda?" Jarrod asks.

"No," I say.

"Does she know that you're planning on going to school in Toronto?"

Silas snaps to look at me so fast I'm worried his head is going to come flying off. "You're going to Toronto? I thought . . ." Silas crosses his arms and stares at the ground, angry.

"Good one, Jarrod."

"You want a say?" Jarrod says, getting up. "Start telling the truth. It's the only way people aren't going to get hurt." He tosses his pop can across the yard. "I'm going to the garage. You guys stay if you want."

"Yeah, you go work!" I yell. "It's all you ever do. You hide from stuff just like the rest of us. You won't do an apprenticeship because you might fail. You'd rather hang out with your dad, where you're safe."

Jarrod turns and looks at me, eyes narrowed, fingers flexing. "You know why I won't go work at that collision shop? You know why I keep missing school?" Jarrod asks, his body stiff. "Ever since Mom died, Dad's been depressed. Lately, when I go to school, he spends the day in bed. But if I work in the garage, he comes and works beside me. He gets happy and sings along to the stereo. I can't take that away from him. I don't mind sacrificing my journeyman's ticket for him, either."

"And I don't mind sacrificing university to have this kid," I say.

"It's not the same," Jarrod counters. "You're asking your girlfriend to make the sacrifice too. Actually, not even asking — you're guilting her into it. That's not fair. I'm going to run the garage one day. I'll be my own boss. In this job, I can do pretty well without a ticket. My situation and your situation are totally different. So don't go attacking me just to make yourself feel better."

I watch Jarrod storm across the alley and disappear into the garage. Silas looks at me, scowling. "Why didn't you tell me you were going to Toronto?"

"I was going to. I only just got the acceptance letter yesterday."

"Sure." Silas picks up a stick and starts hitting the edge of the firepit with it.

"You're just mad that I'm doing something with my life and you're not," I say.

"What would you know about it?" Silas asks.

"All you do is steal stuff, fail classes, and skip school. That's not going to give you a future."

"I do more than that!"

"Yeah, like what?"

"I cook."

"Where? McDonald's?"

"Cody, you're so full of yourself you don't think anyone else has stuff going on."

"Well?" I say. What could Silas possibly be doing that would be as good as going to university? Who would hire such a thief?

"I got set up with a mentor a while back through my social worker," Silas explains. "He gave me a job in his restaurant. A *real* restaurant, where people get dressed up. Right now I mostly wash dishes and do food prep, but I'm learning how to cook. My mentor said he might even send me to SAIT's cooking program if I work hard enough. And one day, I'm going to open my own place."

"Well how was I supposed to know that?" I can't wrap my mind around Silas doing something that he doesn't completely screw up. "You never said anything."

"Yes I did. But you weren't listening." Silas throws the stick and stands up. "You're so wrapped up in your own shit you can't see that other people are doing stuff too." Silas turns his back and stalks into the alley. "I'm out of here."

I sit alone in the backyard for a while, wind running over my skin. Thunder rumbles in the distance. I decide to go. There's nothing for me here.

Chapter 17

Walking down Seventeenth Avenue, I spot a sparkly pink hoodie about a block away. Breaking into a run, I catch up with Carly striding down the street. "Hey girl!" I greet her. "What's up?"

Carly sticks her nose in the air and keeps walking.

"Hey, come on." I grab her arm.

She pulls it free. "Leave me alone."

"Jeez! Is the whole world mad at me?" I ask with a huff. "What's wrong with you?"

"Oh, just your *girlfriend* picking on me because of those photos I tagged. Calling me all kinds of names on Facebook, and you not even saying a word to defend me."

I groan. "I haven't been on Facebook in ages. It was kind of a stupid thing to post, though, don't you think?"

Carly turns her head away and picks up her

pace. I jog to catch up.

"Anyway, it doesn't matter," I continue, "we broke up. Now you and I can —"

"Can what?" Carly snaps. "Have sex again? No way! I'm tired of being used."

"What do you mean? I didn't use you. It was your idea. Both times!"

"And you never called me afterward — again!"

"Your dad —"

"Bullshit." She speeds up once more.

I let out another huff and throw up my hands, striding to keep pace. "Fine. I'm a dick," I say. "I screwed up. I used you to get back at my girlfriend and it blew up in my face."

Carly sniffs. "Knew it."

I take her hand and won't let her tug it back. "Will you at least let me walk with you?"

"I guess."

Her hand relaxes. She lets me interlock my fingers with hers.

We continue that way for a while before Carly reaches up and prods my eyebrow, making me wince. "Silas been planning fun outings again?"

I rub at my new bruises. "No. Just jiu-jitsu class."

"Hmm. Looks like fun."

I grunt. I don't want to think about it.

Twenty minutes later, we get to a small bungalow with toys and tricycles scattered all over the front lawn.

"This isn't your house," I say.

"Nope. This is my aunt's place. I'm babysitting for her tonight. Her regular babysitter is sick."

I kick at a trike with my foot. "How many kids does she have?"

"Three. Twin four-year-old boys and an eighteen-month-old baby girl. They adore me. And all I have to do is put them to bed. Awesome, huh?" Carly gives me a sideways glance. "Want to help?"

I shrug. I've never really babysat. Sure, I've played with little kids — like soccer and hockey. But I haven't looked after them. Stella or Jennie usually got roped into that job. It couldn't be too hard, could it?

"Okay," I answer.

***

The shrieking is like nothing I've ever heard before. It's worse than twenty chainsaws cutting through metal squeaky toys. The high-pitched yowling is paired with gagging, hiccupping, and a zombie movie's worth of snot, tears, and drool. I can't think. It's like I've been cut off from the normal world and warped to the land of brain-crushing racket.

"Take the baby, please!" I beg, holding the toddler at arm's length. She beats her little fists on my arms and squirms.

"Just keep her for two more seconds," Carly pleads. "I'm almost done getting the boys ready for bed."

The twins, Chase and Hunter, jump, yell, and play-fight their way through getting into their pyjamas. They bounce on the bed and try to push each other off. Carly catches each one in turn and slips their clothing on. I don't know how she can operate in such chaos. Finally, with a big shove, Hunter pushes Chase off the bed and into the dresser. Chase howls, his voice a fire engine of pain and fury.

"Is he okay?" I yell, frozen to the spot.

Carly scoops him up and has a look. "It's just a bump. He'll be fine. Give me the baby and I'll get her ready. You take the boys to the bathroom and give Chase a cold cloth." She grabs the still-yowling baby out of my arms and moves toward the other bedroom, calling over her shoulder, "Make sure they brush their teeth and go to the toilet."

In the bathroom, I face the sulking Hunter and sniffing Chase. Chase holds a cold cloth to his head and looks at me wetly. "You look scary."

"So do you," I reply.

"Did you get into a fight?" Hunter asks.

"Yeah, with the last guy who wouldn't get ready for bed. Now brush your teeth and go to the bathroom."

"I gotta get Mr. Fuzzy Bear," Chase says, taking off.

"Nooo!" Hunter howls, running to leave too. "He's mine. I'll punch you!"

I manage to catch Hunter by the shoulder. "No

punching today. Go to the bathroom."

He glares at me.

"Now!" I command.

While Hunter takes a leak, I go to find Chase. He's trotting back with a big brown bear.

"Mr. Fuzzy Bear needs to get ready for bed too," he says

"Fine." I follow him back to the bathroom where I find Hunter dancing around buck naked. "What happened to your PJs?" I ask him.

He shrugs. I look all over the bathroom, but I don't see them. "Do you have any more?"

He nods, smiling, then runs out to get them.

I'm not sure if I should follow him or stay with Chase. Turning back to at least get Chase started on brushing his teeth, I find that he's smeared toothpaste all over the bear.

"No, Chase, toothpaste isn't for toys!"

Chase starts crying. "Don't yell at me!"

"I'm not yelling!" I take a deep breath. "I'll wash it off." I grab a cloth and start to wipe the bear when Hunter screams, "The dresser is tipping! The dresser is tipping!"

I run back to the kids' bedroom and find that Hunter has opened all the drawers of the dresser, unbalancing the thing. Clothes are everywhere and Hunter is moments away from being crushed.

I tip the dresser upright and find a pair of pyjamas, slipping them onto him. Then I herd him back down the hallway and to the bathroom, where I'm greeted by a dripping Mr. Fuzzy Bear as he is lifted out of the toilet and shoved toward my pants. I grab the bear and toss him into the tub, realizing mid-flight that the toilet hasn't been flushed yet. Yuck.

"Chase, go to the bathroom! Hunter, brush your teeth! Now!" I bark.

Both boys stare at me wide-eyed, then run howling out of the room and into Carly's arms. "He's being mean!" they cry.

"Cody, what's going on?" she sighs.

"They . . . they . . ." I don't even know where to begin.

Carly cracks a smile. "I've changed the baby's diaper. Just get her into her sleeper while I deal with the boys. She's in her crib and the outfit is on the change table."

I go to the baby's bedroom. She's standing in her crib, holding the bars, and playing happily with a stuffed giraffe. She turns her little head to see who has walked in. As soon as she spots me, her lip starts quivering. I try to make soothing shush sounds until I sound like I'm a leaking tire. It doesn't help. The ear-bleeding scream starts up again.

Not about to be defeated by a kid who isn't even two, I lift her out of her crib and put her on the change table, still making shushing noises. I hold up her outfit. It's a one-piece thingy. It takes me a few tries to figure out how it goes on. More tries to get both her arms and her legs in without bending them at unnatural angles or having her kick herself out of it again. Then come the snaps. Nothing seems to match up properly. Finally I end up with three snaps that don't seem to connect anywhere. Shrugging, I put her back into the crib. She shrieks even louder.

Carly comes in cooing and picks up the baby, who immediately shuts up. "Do you think you can manage a bedtime story while I get her a bottle?"

I blanch. "I don't know any bedtime stories."

"The kids have books. Just read them one or two."

I go back into the boys' bedroom and find them play-wrestling on one of their beds. I try to speak calmly and not scare them this time. "You guys want a story?"

They both rush off to the bookshelf, throwing every book onto the floor until they find one they like. Unfortunately, it's the same book. I break up the resulting fight and get the kids into bed, then read them a sappy story about a talking tow truck who wants to make friends. I can barely get through it. Just as I finish, Carly comes in, turns off the light, and says goodnight. I follow her to the living room and we sit together on the couch.

"That was a lot of work," I say, moving closer.

She shrugs. "Not really." Carly flips on the TV.

I lay my hands on her shoulders and, since she doesn't move away, I start giving her a massage. She leans into me, rubbing her fingers up and down my leg, making my skin tingle. I kiss the top of her head and she turns her face up to mine, offering her lips. The sound of little feet on linoleum and the click of a doorknob being turned interrupts us. Carly shoots up and runs to the front door. The baby has her hand on the knob and the door partway open. "Want mommy," she sniffles.

"Mommy's at work," Carly says, cuddling her up and taking her back to her room, cooing and talking softly. Twenty impatient, reality-television-filled minutes later, Carly reappears, demanding, "How can you watch that stuff?"

"What took you so long?"

"She didn't want to lie down." Carly shrugs. "That baby is a real escape artist, but I've locked the door now and I think she's on her way to sleep. We should be good."

We get back to kissing and feeling each other up until the mood is rudely broken again by Hunter wanting a glass of water, followed by Chase complaining that Hunter dumped water on him. Then the baby wakes up crying. Just as things settle down once more with the kids, my stomach lets out a rolling growl.

"Sorry," I say. "I didn't have supper."

"Let's order pizza," Carly laughs.

Between us, we have enough money for a large pepperoni and a couple of pops. The guy who delivers it looks a little nervous when I answer the door and scoots away as soon as the money hits his palm. I shut the door with a shake of my head and go to the kitchen.

Carly and I goof around, feeding each other

pizza and talking about all the stupid stories from our long history together. Most of them feature Silas and the great pranks he's done or stupid stunts he's pulled. Like when he tried to light his fart in grade two and was suspended for a week for bringing a lighter to school. Or when he convinced Jarrod that shaving cream was the same as whipped cream and Jarrod ended up looking like a rabid barfing dog. Or the time Silas, Jarrod, and I picked up Carly and her brother in a stolen minivan on our way to Calaway Park, only to crash it a block later. By the end of the pizza, we're both laughing so hard we're barely breathing. "I'm going to go check on the kids," Carly says, getting up. "Be right back."

"When did you say your aunt gets back?" I call down the hallway, wondering if we might have time to get back to what we were doing before the pizza.

Carly returns, breathing hard, arms clutched around her stomach. "Cody, the baby's gone."

Chapter 18

We search all the bedrooms — under furniture, behind dressers, in closets. The house isn't that big and there aren't a lot of hiding places.

"She's not here," Carly sobs.

"Let's look in the living room. Maybe she snuck past us." It's then that I notice the front door is open a crack. My stomach sinks. Chilling anxiety washes through me as I realize what has happened. "Carly . . ." I call.

"Did you find her?" She comes to stand beside me.

I motion to the door. "I forgot to relock it after the pizza came."

"But I told you —"

"I know."

Carly snatches up her shoes. "I've got to find her."

"No." I grab her arm. "You take care of the

boys. I'll look." I slip on my shoes and grab my hoodie. "Which way?"

"I don't know," Carly moans. "The park is that way." She points left. "But her mom goes to work that way." She points right. "And her babysitter lives over there." She points straight ahead. "She's not even two yet, so it's not like she's going to be logical. Just find her. Please."

I head outside. The wind is ripping and the rain is coming down in cold little pellets. The baby must be crying. I listen for the sound. Nothing. The wind whips every noise away, leaving only whooshing in my ears. I turn right and start walking toward her mom's work, then rethink that and go left, back toward the park. Kids like to play, right? But after a block in that direction, I have doubts. Maybe she went to her sitter's.

It's cold. The kid could freeze, just like that three-year-old girl in the States a few years back who managed to open the door and wander out in the middle of the night. She was found dead in a snowbank by the newspaper delivery person the next morning. I don't want to be responsible for something like that. I need help.

Jarrod answers his phone on the second ring. "Oh, it's you," he says without enthusiasm.

"I lost a baby!" I state, eyes darting up and down the road.

"I know. It's all I hear out of you. *Miranda's having an abortion. She's killing my kid.* Blah,

blah, blah. You know Cody, other people have lives too."

"No. You don't understand. I lost a real baby."

"It's just a fetus. It's not even —"

"A toddler, Jarrod. I lost a toddler. I was baby-sitting with Carly and the kid escaped because I didn't lock the front door."

Jarrod pauses. "I'll grab Silas. Where are you?"

Ten minutes later, Jarrod is searching the baby-sitter's route in a classic T-Bird, Silas has taken the park, and I'm on my way toward Seventeenth Avenue — one of the busiest streets in the area. The rain soaks through my hoodie. I shiver, partly from the cold and partly because I'm the stupidest person on the face of the earth. Serious-ly, if I can't even lock a door or get a couple of four-year-olds to brush their teeth, how could I handle an infant of my own? I think of how an-noyed I was about being interrupted by the kids every two seconds. If I had a baby right now, it would have to be my whole life. No girls, no par-ties, no fun. Just drinks of water and pee-soaked teddy bears.

Wow.

My ears throb in the biting wind. I strain to hear the klaxon-alarm howl. Where is that baby? I keep expecting to find her under a tree or behind a car, fist in her mouth, soaked and shivering, smelling of sour milk. I picture myself scooping her up. Be-ing the hero. But all I find is blowing trash and flashing cat's eyes. A dog barks. Traffic roars. I hear a few sirens and wonder if Carly has called the cops yet.

At least Jarrod and Silas are helping, though I don't really know why. I've managed to piss off just about everyone in my life lately. If screwing up was a course, I'd be getting honours.

The steady drone of traffic and the smell of rain and car exhaust becomes stronger. I've reached Seventeenth. Now what? I look down one way, then the other. Shops line both sides of the street, their lights giving off a dirty glow. My phone rings out a tune and I rush to snatch it out of my pocket, nearly dropping it in the process.

"News?" I ask, desperate.

It's Silas. His voice is flat. "We found her. She's dead."

My ears ring. I go stiff. "What?" I gasp.

"Just joking," he yips. "The kid's fine. Jarrod found her. We're hanging out with Carly."

I let lose a few swears before hanging up and pounding back to the house. Everyone is in the living room. Jarrod has the baby on his knee, bouncing her. She has a cherry lollipop in her fist and her face is covered with sticky red goo, but she looks all right. She even gives me a lopsided grin.

"Carly," I gasp, trying to catch my breath. "I'm sorry."

"You're so stupid," Carly says, smacking me.

Silas hits me too.

"What's that for?" I ask, rubbing my arm.

"I agree with Carly," he says.

"Me too," Jarrod puts in.

"Do I get a vote?" I ask.

"Depends," Jarrod says.

"On what?"

Silas crosses his arms. "Admit you're not the big shot you think you are."

"Stop being so preachy," Jarrod adds.

"Stop being dumb," Carly says, looking at the baby.

"Okay, I'm sorry. I suck," I reply, looking at Silas and Jarrod. "I've been way too full of myself and my problems. I can barely live my life, let alone tell you guys how to run yours." I go over and pat the baby on the head, getting sticky in the process. "And I'm sorry, Carly," I say to her. "I should have locked the door."

She eyes me, still scowling.

"And phoned you too," I add.

Carly nods, her expression softening.

Chapter 19

The next day after school, I'm clutching super-perfumed grocery-store flowers, plastic wrap rustling. I stride up to the Blakes' front door. The curtain in Miranda's room flutters, then lies still. I reach up to knock on the door but it opens before my knuckles hit it. Adam stands there, teeth clenched.

"What do you want?" he demands.

"I need to talk to Miranda," I reply.

"No way." He spreads his feet wide and blocks the way. Adam's left eye is a purply-green and his cheek is slightly swollen. It must have been from our fight.

Guilt makes me bow my head. "Sorry about the bruises."

Adam reaches up to touch his face. He eyes me seriously. "I can't tell if I hurt you. You were beaten up pretty badly already."

I crack a smile. "Yeah, you got me. I've been feeling it all day."

"Well, I did warn you," Adam says.

"Yes, you did," I agree, "and I hurt your sister. That's why I have to talk with her."

He shakes his head. "You can't see her."

"Adam!" Miranda calls from somewhere above. "Let him in."

"But Dad said —" Adam calls back.

"Dad's not here."

Adam motions me in with a flick of his head. "She's in her room. I'm sure you know where that is."

I try to keep my grin to myself.

"Be quick, our parents are only picking up supper," he advises.

Miranda's sitting on her bed in loose-fitting jogging pants and a baggy t-shirt. She looks pale and tired. I guess all the stress has finally taken a toll on her. I know it has on me. I feel like crap. Inside and out.

"Cody, I have something to tell you," she says, looking serious.

"Me too," I say, handing her the flowers. "I'm sorry for being a jerk. For pushing you to do something you weren't ready to do. For not listening to you."

Miranda holds the flowers close to her chest, their gaudy colour bright against her skin. "So, you're okay with it now?" she asks, doubtful.

I shake my head. "No."

Miranda frowns. "What then?"

I sit on the bed, across from her, our knees inches away. "I still don't agree with abortion. It's wrong and I can't change my mind on that."

"Cody . . ." Her lips narrow. "You can't change my mind either. It's too —"

"Hear me out," I interrupt.

"I have," she snaps. "Lots."

"But —"

"You can't force-feed me your opinion."

I get up. Pace. "Yeah, neither can you."

Miranda snorts. "Obviously."

"But will you listen anyway?" I huff.

"Fine. Two seconds. Go."

"I don't agree with abortion, but I don't think us having a kid is right either."

"Huh?" She shakes her head.

"I can't handle a baby. There's no way. I couldn't even have a girlfriend without messing it up and you are way less work than a kid."

"So what does that mean?"

"I don't know." I shrug, almost as confused as she is. "I guess, well, if you're going to have the abortion, I'll go along with it. I'll support you, because even though it isn't right, it's right for us."

Miranda sighs. "Cody, you're making almost no sense."

"I'm trying to explain."

"So, let me get this straight, you won't fight me on this abortion anymore because babies are more

142

work than girlfriends." She lets go a sly smile.

I nod. "Something like that. The thing is, whenever I pictured my life before all this, it was all about university. You know, chasing girls, going to parties, and," Jennie's talk about her brother shoves its way into my mind, "studying," I end a little lamely.

"You were going to dump me to chase girls even before this happened?" Miranda throws her pillow at me.

I catch it and bring it back to her, sitting down across from her again. "That's just it. I didn't even see us together after this year. I don't know if you've noticed, but I'm a little bit —"

"Self-centred?" she snaps.

"Well," I shrug. "Yeah, I guess. I was going to say 'into girls.'"

"Same thing," Miranda shrugs.

"I just want to do the right thing," I explain. "For you. For us."

"So what's the right thing?" she asks, not even looking at me.

"Not having this kid right now."

"Good. I'm glad you came to your senses."

"Miranda," I reach out to her. "Just let me go with you. To the abortion clinic. I want to be there to see this through to the end. I want some, I don't know, closure."

Miranda immediately shuts down. Her face becomes an emotionless mask. The flowers crush into her lap. "You can't," she whispers.

"I won't try to stop you," I beg. "Come on. Please."

"You can't," she repeats, still not meeting my eyes.

"Why?" I'm getting angry. I'm tired of pleading to be a part of this. I have rights, even if they aren't written into Canadian law.

"Because it's done," she says, eyes flashing with barely-held tears. "I've already had it."

"Liar!" I roar, jumping up and punching the air. "You liar!"

"I had to, Cody."

"But you said . . ." I counter, not quite believing what she's saying. "You *promised* you'd tell me!"

"You were being unreasonable! Besides, my dad said if he ever saw you again, he'd —"

"This was between *us*, not our parents!" I scream, pointing my finger in her face.

"You're the one who told them!" Miranda returns, angry, knocking my hand aside. "If you hadn't, I might have let you come."

I shake my head. This is so messed up. "You never cared about what I wanted!" I yell.

"Ditto!" she returns.

"At least I'm trying to see your point of view!" I counter.

"How the hell was I supposed to know you'd changed your mind? I'm not psychic. Besides, my mom came with me. Still," she shudders. "It was awful."

"Good," I mutter, turning away.

"Thanks," Miranda snarls. "I think you better go."

I walk to the bedroom door, then freeze, hand on the knob. "What was it like?" I ask.

"Like being scraped clean. I made me feel so . . . empty."

A gong of sadness echoes inside me. "I feel empty too," I say.

"I'm sorry, Cody."

"No you're not." I want to turn the knob. Leave her room. Leave this city. But I can't move. Can't function under the blow of this news. It's over. It's all over.

The bed creaks. Her socks crackle with static from the rug. Fingers squeeze my shoulder. Arms circle my waist. The scent of lilacs floats past my nose.

"I am sorry," she says. "I wish it could have been different. But now it feels like I can plan my life again. Like I'm not standing still, waiting." She puts her hand on my chest. "What about you?"

I clench my teeth. Turn to face her. Pull her hands from my body and step back. "Miranda, I don't want to see you again. Not after this. It's . . . too much."

She nods, her brown hair half-covering her bright hazel eyes. "Me either. I'm scared that every time I look at you, I'll remember . . ." she hugs her arms around her torso, "and I don't want to. It's too hard."

Chapter 20

On the bus ride home, all I can think about is Toronto. No one is going to stop me. I'm starting a new life. I know I'm not the brightest guy on the planet, or the most talented — except at maybe landing in trouble. But I will never, ever, allow myself to be in this situation again. I'll make sure of it.

I get off the bus and walk into the house, my new life playing out in my head. It takes me a minute to realize that the kitchen table is packed. It looks like one of those intervention shows, except I'm not on drugs. Grandma smiles, as do all my aunts. My mom waves. Stella looks away. Uncle Tom comes to a stand. I glare at Jennie. She glares right back at me.

I start to take off my jacket, head to my room. Hide.

"Don't bother," Uncle Tom says. "Let's go."

***

Dry prairie grass whispers in the warm wind. The red sky is spiked with the orange rays of sinking sun. I stand beside my uncle, breathing in the closing blooms of prairie crocus and dusty-green sage. Our gaze is set over the Weaslehead and beyond it, to the Tsuu T'ina reserve.

"So you got a girl pregnant, huh?" my uncle finally says, sitting on a bench and patting the empty spot beside him.

We've been hiking for about an hour, watching a peregrine falcon soaring overhead, and being squeaked at by numerous Richardson's ground squirrels — though that may have been directed at the falcon.

I sit, but I don't look at him. My gaze is still on the sparkling water down below on the mud flats. Ducks flap and race, sending out long streams of white water behind them.

I let out a frustrated sigh. "I knew Jennie would rat me out."

"She didn't," my uncle says.

"Then Stella?"

"Nope."

I'm out of suspects. "Who?"

"Your dad."

I spin and stare at my uncle. "What?"

"He was worried about you. Thought you might take what he said the wrong way. Though why in

the hell you'd ask him for advice is beyond me."
Uncle Tom sighs, his gnarled fingers rubbing his
wrinkle-folded face.

"Well, it's my last time." I scowl. "I nearly got
my head taken off with a golf club."

"You could have asked me," Uncle Tom says.
"I'm here for you." He opens his arms wide.
"We're all here for you."

"You mean my family?" I ask, casting my gaze
far. "I know that."

"Sure, them. But he is too." Uncle Tom points
up at the wheeling falcon, eyes scouring the
ground for a tasty rodent. "And that guy," he indi-
cates a young ground squirrel looking us with a
cocked head, then points to another one a bit further off. "But not him. I don't trust him. This is
your land, Cody, it looks after you."

"Okay . . ." I say, wondering if Uncle Tom is
going to start telling me a legend like he does
sometimes when he's having trouble expressing
his ideas.

"Toronto is pretty far away," he says instead.

"Your point being?" I reply. I know I'm being difficult. I just don't want to be talked out of
this. I want to get away. I want to be out on my
own. Away from friends who know how stupid I
am and jiu-jitsu teachers waiting for apologies.
Twin brothers who will never forgive me, and my
family, who gossip about my every failure while
rubbing their hands waiting for the next screw-up.

"Your mom will miss you," Uncle Tom says.

"So will Stella and your aunts. Me. Jennie."

"Jennie won't miss me. She hates me."

"She loves you. She kept your secret. Wouldn't tell us anything. Well . . . not about the pregnancy thing anyway. Not even when we asked her outright."

I snort. "Give me a break!"

"Seriously." Uncle Tom puts up his hands, callused palms out. "I couldn't believe it myself. I mean, that girl sure can run at the mouth."

I shake my head.

"She doesn't want you to go to Toronto," he says.

"She doesn't want me to go to university."

"She's worried that she'll lose you like she lost her brother."

I scowl at the darkening sky. "No one thinks I can do it. You guys just wait for me to mess up. In Toronto, I can get away from all that."

"You're wrong. We're not waiting for you to mess up. We're watching you learn — celebrating when you succeed, and giving you a nudge when you need a little direction."

"Like now?"

"You got a girl pregnant and you're planning on moving across the country — so yeah, like now."

"She had an abortion."

"And?"

"It sucked," I say, fighting to cover the shaking that gets between my words. "But it's over and there's nothing I can do about it except make sure that it never happens again."

"What about the other thing?"

"I got accepted to the University of Calgary too."

"So . . ."

"If I stay, I'll never hear the end of it."

Uncle Tom laughs. "Oh, come on! You're not that interesting. It will blow over."

I frown. "I need my space."

Uncle Tom pats me on the shoulder. "Then live with me. I could use the company. It could be a real bachelor pad. You know, socks on the door-knobs whenever we have . . . um . . . visitors."

"What about Jennie?"

"Are you kidding?" Uncle Tom says. "My place has been a Jennie-free zone for years. I don't like people talking about me either. You have to re-member — your aunts are my sisters."

The peregrine falcon dives, raking up an un-lucky ground squirrel. The sun stains the sky purple. I lean back on the bench. Stretch my legs out. Cross my arms over my chest. "Fine. I'll stay. I'll go to the University of Calgary." I suck in a big lungful of sweet prairie air. It tastes like home. "Happy?"

"Sure, whatever. It's your decision." Uncle Tom gets up, his knees popping. "Man, I'm starv-ing. Want to grab a burger or something?"

I follow him down the path to the parking lot, opening the door to his truck.

Getting in and starting the engine, he chuckles.

"Did I ever tell you about the time I took off for Los Angeles back in the eighties? That was a crazy time. Wasn't much older than you. Needed some space away from my sisters — you know. And there was this girl. Man, she was cute."

And, weird as it is, with Toronto evaporating before my eyes and Uncle Tom full into another story from his past, I have to say I'm pretty happy. Not completely sure why, but things feel right. Besides, I hear there's some pretty cute girls at the U of C. And Carly's here. Maybe I can make things right with her.